"My room has a private entrance."

The silence arced between them, intense and urgent, as compelling as the fire blazing in his eyes. With him, she would find sweet fulfillment.

It would be bliss. And it would be based on lies. Tomorrow always came and with it the reckoning she'd come to expect. Then whatever they'd shared would be lost, one more thing to remember with regret....

"What troubles you so?" he asked.

"Us," she admitted. "And all that it implies."

"Which is?"

She turned from his scrutiny. "I don't know."

He nodded as if he understood. "Sometimes things move too fast. There are too many questions."

The questions pertained to her. She clenched her hands and wished she could tell him *everything*— all her worries, her yearnings, her dreams.

He let off the brake and made the turn onto the road home. His home, not hers. She must remember that.

Dear Reader,

Your best bet for coping with April showers is to run—not walk—to your favorite retail outlet and check out this month's lineup. We'd like to highlight popular author Laurie Paige and her new miniseries SEVEN DEVILS. Laurie writes, "On my way to a writers' conference in Denver, I spotted the Seven Devils Mountains. This had to be checked out! Sure enough, the rugged, fascinating land proved to be ideal for a bunch of orphans who'd been demanding that their stories be told." You won't want to miss *Showdown!*, the second book in the series, which is about a barmaid and a sheriff destined for love!

Gina Wilkins dazzles us with *Conflict of Interest,* the second book in THE McCLOUDS OF MISSISSIPPI series, which deals with the combustible chemistry between a beautiful literary agent and her ruggedly handsome and reclusive author. Can they have some fun without love taking over the relationship? Don't miss Marilyn Pappano's *The Trouble with Josh,* which features a breast cancer survivor who decides to take life by storm and make the most of everything—but she never counts on sexy cowboy Josh Rawlins coming into the mix.

In Peggy Webb's *The Mona Lucy,* a meddling but well-meaning mother attempts to play Cupid to her son and a beautiful artist who is painting her portrait. Karen Rose Smith brings us *Expecting the CEO's Baby,* an adorable tale about a mix-up at the fertility clinic and a marriage of convenience between two strangers. And in Lisette Belisle's *His Pretend Wife,* an accident throws an ex-con and an ex-debutante together, making them discover that rather than enemies, they just might be soul mates!

As you can see, we have a variety of stories for our readers, which explore the essentials—life, love and family. Stay tuned next month for six more top picks from Special Edition!

Sincerely,

Karen Taylor Richman
Senior Editor

Please address questions and book requests to:
Silhouette Reader Service
U.S.: 3010 Walden Ave., P.O. Box 1325, Buffalo, NY 14269
Canadian: P.O. Box 609, Fort Erie, Ont. L2A 5X3

Laurie Paige

SHOWDOWN!

SPECIAL EDITION™

Published by Silhouette Books

America's Publisher of Contemporary Romance

To the Redding bunch—for the laughs, the sharing and the wedding from you-know-where. It was a riot!

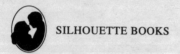 SILHOUETTE BOOKS

ISBN 0-373-24532-7

SHOWDOWN!

Copyright © 2003 by Olivia M. Hall

This edition published by arrangement with Harlequin Books S.A.

® and TM are trademarks of Harlequin Books S.A., used under license. Trademarks indicated with ® are registered in the United States Patent and Trademark Office, the Canadian Trade Marks Office and in other countries.

Visit Silhouette at www.eHarlequin.com

Printed in U.S.A.

Books by Laurie Paige

LAURIE PAIGE

"One of the nicest things about writing romances is researching locales, careers and ideas. In the interst of authenticity, most writers will try anything…once." Along with her writing adventures, Laurie has been a NASA engineer, a past president of the Romance Writers of America, a mother and a grandmother. She was twice a Romance Writers of America RITA® Award finalist for Best Traditional Romance and has won awards from *Romantic Times* for Best Silhouette Special Edition and Best Silhouette.

DALTON FAMILY TREE

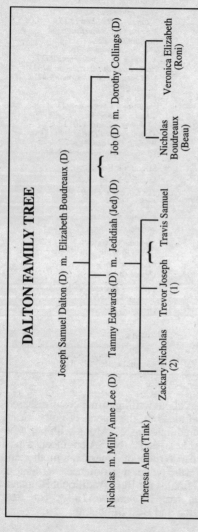

Joseph Samuel Dalton (D) m. Elizabeth Boudreaux (D)

Nicholas m. Milly Anne Lee (D)   Tammy Edwards (D) m. Jedidiah (Jed) (D)   Job (D) m. Dorothy Collings (D)

Theresa Anne (Tink)

Zackary Nicholas (2)   Trevor Joseph (1)   Travis Samuel

Nicholas Boudreaux (Beau)   Veronica Elizabeth (Roni)

(1) *Something To Hide* (part of *Claiming His Own*)
(2) *Showdown!* (SE #1532)

Dorothy Collings died after eight years of marriage and Job's significant other at time of death was Camilla White Feather Diego, whose son, Seth, was taken in by Uncle Nick (and given the Dalton name) when Camilla died in an avalanche with Job, Jed and Tammy.

{ twins

D deceased

Chapter One

"Last one," Zack Dalton reminded Lady Luck, but without much hope the fabled lady would have a change of heart and smile on him.

Huh. His luck with females had been pretty sour lately. A tang of bitterness like the aftertaste of fine wine gone to vinegar lingered on his tongue. He ignored it and the accompanying pang in his heart. He'd trusted one female with that organ and had had it handed back to him last summer when his fiancée had visited relatives in Denver, met some rich guy and married him on the spot.

So much for trust, loyalty and true love.

His uncle Nick said all things happened for the best. Looking at it that way, he figured he'd gotten off easy, heart and pride dinged but repairable.

He fed his last quarter into the slot machine, pushed the button and watched the wheels spin. They came up zilch. Okay, so he wasn't destined to be rich. That probably was for the best, he consoled himself philosophically, then chuckled at his little jest.

Glancing at the clock, he saw it was midnight. The reason he was at the slots was simple. Las Vegas was truly a city that never slept. It wouldn't let *him* catch any zzz's, either. Too many lights, too many people, too much noise at all hours.

His duty here was done and he could start home tomorrow. He'd better try for some rest, assuming he could find the elevator that would take him from the casino level to his floor far above the neon sparkle of the famous strip. He glanced around, searching for a landmark as a guide.

"You dropped a coin, sir," a polite voice, very feminine, very soft, spoke from behind his left shoulder.

He swiveled around on the stool and gazed into eyes rimmed by false lashes so long he wondered how the cocktail waitress could lift her eyelids. The lashes cast such deep shadows he couldn't tell what color her eyes were. The rest of her makeup was just as exaggerated, giving her a fake tan and rosily blushing cheeks that were obviously painted on. Dark roots showed along the uneven part in her blond hair.

While he liked his women more natural, sort of outdoorsy, his interest was piqued by the beauty spot a half inch from one corner of her mouth. Her lips had a full, soft look in spite of the thick lipstick. The fullness coupled with the tiny mole gave her mouth a sort of vulnerability that surprised him.

Even more surprising was his urge to touch her, as if he needed to be sure she was real. He had an instant, equally strong desire to kiss her.

Whoa! He hadn't had *that* many beers, at least he didn't think he had.

"Sir?" she said in that soft voice so at odds with her been-there-done-that appearance.

He took the quarter, dropped it in the slot and hit the spin button as he watched her deliver a drink to a man three machines down. From this view, she looked great.

Her outfit was cut into a provocative drape that left a lot of bare skin. She had smooth shoulders and a small waist, slender hips and firm thighs clad in fishnet hose.

He paused to admire the thighs.

A bell clanged and the sound of falling coins assailed his ears. Other players looked at him, some with envy, some with smiles. Zack frowned at his machine. When he looked around again, the waitress was gone.

"Here, you'll need a bucket," the soft voice said, speaking from his right this time. A plastic bucket was plunked down on the narrow ledge between the slots.

"Thanks," he said, but she was already gone.

A number was flashing on the slot display. His brain seemed swathed in cotton as he tried to divide four into six hundred and come up with the amount of his winnings.

"Boy, howdy, 150 smackers," the man on his left said jovially, giving him the answer. "Not bad for a couple of hours' work, huh?"

Actually it was a nice bonus, considering he'd had the unpleasant job of returning an escaped prisoner, captured in Idaho, to Vegas. The deputies had drawn lots on Monday to see who had to do the task and he'd won. Or lost, according to how one looked at it.

Speaking of winning, he realized he owed the waitress a big tip. As he rose, four couples, boisterous and merry, jostled their way down the aisle. One of them hit his arm. Six hundred quarters hit the floor.

"Oops, sorry," one of the happy group said, not the least bit remorseful. "Hey, great win."

Five minutes of chaos reigned while they scrambled to pick up the coins and toss them back into his bucket. Since there was no room for him to join them, he stood still and watched. The men and women, bobbing up and down as they worked, reminded him of the chickens his uncle Nick insisted on raising back at the Seven Devils Ranch.

He patiently waited until the noisy couples finished and left, apologizing loudly for the trouble they'd caused. When the aisle cleared, a shapely derriere was directly in front of him. The waitress was on her knees, retrieving coins from under the adjacent row of slots.

Zack's eyes widened, then narrowed as he stared at her left thigh just below the skimpy, high-cut costume. He took three steps, then bent down as if he, too, was looking for quarters. From the vantage of a foot away, he could see her upper thigh where it joined the delectable curve of her hip.

Yep, a scar was discernible under the fishnet. He inched closer. The scar was jagged and three-pointed. His lungs stopped working while his heart went into overdrive.

"My gosh," he muttered, blinking in amazement. Talk about luck; he couldn't believe this. Lifting one finger, he traced the outline—

"Aaaiii," the waitress squealed, straightening abruptly.

"Back up, buddy," a security cop ordered, appearing out of nowhere and grabbing him by the collar. Zack was strong-armed to a standing position. The cop's partner stood close by, alert for trouble.

"It's okay," he assured the cop. "She's my cousin."

The security men looked at the woman.

"I've never seen him before in my life," she declared in shocked tones, the painted eyebrows rising indignantly as she moved away from him, the delectable lips compressed in a narrow line.

"That's true, but I know you," Zack explained, speaking in reasonable tones and tamping the excitement down. "That scar on your butt, uh, buttock, uh, thigh is a dead giveaway."

"We'll take care of him," the cop told the woman. She disappeared into the crowd while Zack was held and questioned by the patrol. "You staying here?" the older one asked.

"Yeah."

"You need help getting to your room?"

"I'm not leaving," he told them firmly. "Now that I've found Uncle Nick's daughter, I've got to take her home. To the ranch," he added in case they misunderstood where he meant. "Seven Devils Mountains. Idaho."

"Detank," one of the security patrol said.

"Right. You want me to report it?" the other man asked. "It's Friday. You're supposed to leave early tonight."

The first man sighed. "I'll do it when I sign out."

Zack realized the futility of protesting as they led him to a private room down a narrow corridor off the elevator area. He was vaguely amused as he thought of possible headlines: Visiting cop busted in a casino for looking at a woman's—

The rest of the thought was lost as the door slammed behind him and locked. He realized two things. One, "detank" was a place for inebriated clients to sleep it off. Two, they thought he fit that description.

Apparently he hadn't explained himself well enough. He was now trapped in the proverbial padded cell. A leather sofa and chair were the only furnishings. He sat down to wait for some form of rescue, his bucket of quarters still clenched in one hand.

One thing he noticed right away: it was quiet in

here. No traffic. No sirens. No bursts of laughter or strange voices outside his bedroom door. Just blissful silence.

He yawned. In the four days he'd been on this trip, he hadn't had a full night's sleep due to all the racket.

Hannah "Honey" Carrington finished her shift at two in the morning. She turned in her cash, then went to the locker room. After tucking the money apron onto a shelf, she changed shoes and pulled a shirt and long skirt over her working outfit. Grabbing her purse, she headed out, glad to be going home.

"Hey, Bert," she said to the security guard who was also going off duty.

"Hey, Honey," the guard said.

"Say, what happened to the guy who was in the casino?" she asked. "The one who said he was my cousin," she added with a sardonic smile. She'd heard a few lines in her time, but that had been a new one.

Bert frowned. "I don't know. Bill took care of it." Alarm spread over his face. "Uh-oh."

"What?"

"Bill. He got a call just after we left you. His wife is having a baby. That's why he was supposed to leave early. I sure hope—" He broke off and headed toward the elevators at a near run.

Although instinct said she should go home and not get involved, Honey trailed after him. The tall lanky stranger had been polite in his dealings with her. He was handsome, and she'd found him interesting. There had been an amused gentleness about him—as if he laughed at life's vagaries.

Then he'd made the peculiar crack about being cousins. That had put her on guard and reminded her that, for her own good, she should be more cynical about people.

When Bert unlocked the door to the holding room, she followed him inside. A soft snore greeted them.

The stranger was sound asleep on the sofa, his bucket of change balanced on his stomach, rising and falling with each breath.

"At least he isn't climbing the walls," Bert muttered under his breath, then called to the detained customer. "Sir? Sir? It's time to go. Rise and shine."

The stranger awoke at once, grabbed the bucket before it toppled and rose to a sitting position. "What's up?"

"You can go," Bert told him. "Do you remember where you're staying?"

"Sure. Here. Room 2008." He pulled the card key from his pocket as if to prove it.

"Good. The elevator is this way."

The stranger spotted her hovering behind the security guard. His smile was quick and delighted. Dazzling. His eyes were a deep, true blue, his hair dark, a little long and enticingly tousled as it swept over his forehead in a deep wave. An odd tension filled her when he looked her way.

"Hi, cousin," he said.

"Sorry, I'm not your cousin."

Had she not learned to be skeptical of people's motives, she might have believed he thought she really was his cousin. There was an engaging openness and confidence about the stranger, as if he knew where he belonged and was content in that knowledge. She could envy him that.

For the briefest moment, the despair and sense of vulnerability, of always being held hostage to the whims of a dark fate, loomed over her. She felt utterly alone in the world.

Poor little lonely one, she mocked the self-pity. She had an aunt and a cousin, not that they were close, but still, they existed. She had a brother, but she didn't know where he was or even if he was dead or alive.

As an undercover agent with the FBI, Adam had important work to do, work that often put him in danger and out of immediate contact. She'd learned to be self-sufficient.

"You have the scar," the stranger said.

The flesh on her thigh tingled. "I've had that since I was a child."

"I know. Since you were three," he said.

Honey's mouth gaped. How had he known that?

"It's time to go," Bert interjected, checking the time, then moving toward the door. "Do you need help getting to your room?"

"No, thanks." The stranger turned his probing gaze back to her. "Are you off work now?"

She nodded warily.

"Good. We need to talk." He pulled on his boots

and rose in one fluid motion, standing a good six inches over Bert. "How about something to eat? Your friend can join us." He pointed to the security guard.

"I'm going home," Bert said in no uncertain terms.

"Me, too." She edged toward the door.

The stranger frowned, then reached into his back pocket and brought out his wallet. To her surprise, he showed them a badge. "Zackary Nicholas Dalton," he introduced himself.

Bert studied the badge. "You're a deputy sheriff? From Idaho?"

"Right. I had official business here, which is finished. I'd planned to start home in the morning, uh, this morning." He spoke to her. "I really need to talk to you before I go. This is serious."

Seeing Bert check the time again, Honey shook her head. "I'm beat. And I'm not your cousin."

"You could be. Do you remember where you were born? Or who your parents were?"

His words gave her pause. She and Adam had been orphaned when she was three and her brother thirteen. Their father had been killed in a bar shoot-out through no fault of his own; he and a friend happened to be in the wrong place at the wrong time. Two years later their mother had died of a rare antibiotic-resistant pneumonia.

"Well?" the lawman demanded.

"Of course I do," she said firmly.

"Are they alive?"

She stopped, startled by the question, her eyes locking with the stranger's.

"Ah," he said, reading her correctly. "They're not."

"That…that doesn't mean anything."

"Do you remember them?" the deputy persisted.

"Not my father, but I remember my mother. I do," she said when he raised straight dark eyebrows over skeptical eyes. "A few things."

"How old were you when she died?"

Honey nearly answered, but stopped in time. Her past was none of this man's business.

Bert gestured impatiently. "Let's go." He ushered them from the holding room, slammed the door, then gazed at her in uncertainty.

"Go home," she told the guard. "I'll be fine."

"Where can we talk?" the visiting deputy asked, blocking her escape with the hand holding the bucket of quarters.

"We can't." She hurried after the guard. "Leave me alone, or I'll call security again."

"Listen, I know this sounds weird, but my cousin really does have a three-pointed scar on her leg. She fell on broken glass when she was three. A few months later she was taken from the scene of a car wreck. That was shortly before her fourth birthday."

"Taken?"

"Kidnapped. Her mother died in the wreck on a lonely stretch of highway. Some pervert took the child."

Honey was aghast. "How long ago was this?"

"Twenty-two years. Tink would be twenty-six her next birthday. How old are you?"

A wave of panic rushed over her, as if she might indeed be this long-lost cousin, as if her own past had been a lie. She shook off the idea. "Twenty-five, but I'm not the person you're looking for." She heard the note of desperation in her voice. Her life was complicated enough without having to deal with this man's search for his cousin. "I'm not. Really. It's impossible."

"Uncle Nick had a heart attack," the deputy told her, sorrow darkening his eyes. "He kept muttering about Tink while he was unconscious. The family—I have twin brothers and three cousins—decided to try to find her. Are you sure about your past?"

"Well…yes. I'm sorry about your uncle," she said sincerely.

"Yeah, he's the greatest," he said, his eyes looking her over as if searching for some truth that should be evident. "He took in six orphans and raised us as his own. Even after losing his wife and child, his care for us never faltered, not once."

His tale was similar to her own story, yet so different. As orphans, she and Adam had lived with their only relative, an aunt who had never wanted them and had never let them forget it. Honey sighed and blocked the thought.

"I'm really sorry. I have to go." She hurried off,

leaving the handsome stranger watching her with a thoughtful look in his gorgeous blue eyes.

At her one-room studio apartment, she prepared for bed, aware of the weariness that seemed to pulsate from every bone in her body. Clomping around in stiletto heels for several hours was extremely tiring. She hated the smoke and noise of the casino, too. In fact, there was very little she enjoyed about her life at the moment.

For some reason, the image of the handsome lawman came to her—the confidence of his smile, the humor in his eyes, the love he obviously had for his uncle. She sensed an innate integrity in him, the same as her brother had, and kindness…

Unexpected tears burned her eyes, startling her. Good heavens, she really was going off the deep end since encountering the deputy with the heavenly eyes.

Ah, well, this, too, would pass. Besides, she wasn't normally a crybaby. Neither tears nor wishes had ever changed a thing in her life.

After brushing her teeth, she got out her laptop computer and checked her e-mails.

Her breath stopped momentarily when she saw the coded one from her brother. She quickly opened the mail, which appeared to be an advertisement of an upcoming sale. The date and hours of the sale were a reference to the time her brother would call. That he used this method of contact meant he was in deep, deep cover and in danger.

And so was she.

No matter what happened she wouldn't return to a "safe" house. She'd lived there just before leaving L.A. Being "safe" had been the same as being in prison—no visitors, no calls, no going out.

No, thanks.

Her aunt's favorite punishment had been to lock her and Adam in the bedroom and leave them for hours. As a child, Honey had often worried that they would be forgotten. Adam had told her they had to be brave, so she'd learned to conceal the fear. But it had been scary.

She closed her eyes as the memories swamped her with the old familiar anguish. After a moment she resolutely shook off the despair. Adam could take care of himself. She could do the same. No one would ever associate a bleached-blond waitress with the real Hannah Smith.

No! She couldn't think of herself as Hannah Smith. She was using a fake name with a fake ID. For now and the foreseeable future, she was Honey Carrington.

The deputy was waiting at the service entrance when Honey arrived for work at six the next evening. She hesitated when she saw him, recalling a movie about a stalker she'd recently seen on TV.

"It's okay," he said, smiling and holding up his hands. "I'm harmless. I wondered if we could talk."

"I thought you were on your way home."

He gave her a smile. "Well, the best-laid plans and

all that.'' He fell into step beside her. ''Do you have time for a cup of coffee?''

She clenched her hands as indecision ate at her. Her brother had called. He wanted her in a safe house on the East Coast. She'd refused. He'd been furious with her.

His cover had been blown a month ago. That was why she'd had to give up her position with the dance troupe that had brought her from Los Angeles to Las Vegas to perform at the casino theater and take on the disguise as a waitress.

In a scandal that appeared to be larger than the Rampart case, the FBI had been called in by the LAPD chief of Internal Affairs to infiltrate a police crime ring. Her brother had drawn the assignment.

Now the gang knew of her and wanted to use her to force Adam into the open, according to his contact within the rogue-cop group. He had warned her succinctly of what would happen if either of them was found.

Naturally she would do whatever it took to protect her brother. The stranger was a cop, but far removed from the L.A. crime scene. He offered the perfect escape. Did she dare take it?

Adam thought she should. He'd checked out the deputy and found him to be legit. Apparently the Daltons were a very respected ranching family that went back for generations, according to Adam's research, which he'd reported to her an hour ago.

If she wouldn't accept protection, then she should

go where no one would easily find her. Who, Adam had argued, would think to look for her in Idaho? He'd made a good point. She'd thought of little else during her time off.

"Yes, I have a few minutes," she said to the deputy, putting off the moment when she had to make the difficult decision.

"Can you find the coffee shop? I seem to go around in circles here."

She had to smile. "The casino's designed that way. You have to go past the slots and gaming tables to get anywhere else." She led the way to the café. "Tell me about your cousin," she said when they were seated.

"There isn't much to tell. She disappeared when she was three and a half from a car wreck, which killed her mother. Tink was nowhere to be found when help arrived."

"Maybe she wandered away and got lost," Honey said. A vision of the child roaming dazed and confused through a dark forest, perhaps searching for her father, flashed on her mental screen. Sympathy stirred in her.

He shrugged. "All we know for sure is that someone else was at the site. The cops found tire tracks and boot prints, a child's prints next to them. A man in a pickup had come through town that morning. He stopped for gas. The station owner recalled his license plate was from California. How did you get the scar on your leg?"

Honey blinked at the change in subject. "My aunt

said my cousin pushed me and I fell on a broken bottle.''

''Your aunt?''

Honey nodded, her mind still on the little girl who had disappeared. She knew what it was like to feel lost and bewildered. Abandoned. It was a scary thing for a child.

''What happened to your parents?'' he demanded, leaning forward over the table to stare at her intently.

''They died.''

''How? When?''

''My father was accidentally shot in a bar. My mother got sick a couple of years later. It was a long time ago,'' she said to forestall the questions she could see coming. ''I wasn't quite four. I don't remember anything except my mother left for the hospital and never came back.''

''The woman who said she was your aunt—''

''She *is* my aunt.''

''Does she have children?''

Honey tried to figure out what he was driving at. ''A son. He's six years older than I am. Aunt May couldn't have more children.''

''Hmm,'' the deputy said as if this was significant.

''What?''

''What if she wanted another child, a little girl to complete her family? What if she was willing to pay?'' the deputy asked earnestly.

Honey kept a straight face. Her aunt had hated having her and her brother in the house. She'd hated spending any money on them, even though she got a check from welfare each month to support the two orphans.

"I don't think that's likely," she told him wryly, wishing she had been the loved and wanted little girl his words described, wishing she could have had a family like this man apparently had. If wishes were wings...

"Come to the ranch with me and talk to Uncle Nick," he urged. "You might remember something. If nothing else, I can promise you a great vacation. Mountain air. Beautiful views. Quiet. No one to bother you."

Did he realize how appealing that sounded? "I have to work." She paused, knowing she couldn't use him for her own purposes but already regretting the loss. "I'm sorry about your cousin. I hope you find her."

"Thanks."

He let her go, his expression thoughtful. Honey was aware of the scar on her thigh as she walked away.

Idaho. She'd studied maps of it last night. The state seemed far from everything she'd ever known. He, or the uncle he was so fond of, had a ranch there. It sounded like heaven, a sanctuary for the weary soul.

Peace. Quiet. Safety.

Oh, yes, she was tempted, so very tempted.

Chapter Two

By ten o'clock Zack knew the layout of the casino and had a plan. If there was the slightest chance the waitress was Tink—and in addition to the scar, there was enough about her past to justify the possibility—he couldn't leave without trying to convince her to come home with him and at least talk to Uncle Nick.

He waited for her next to the locker-room door where he hoped she would soon appear. It should be her dinner hour about now.

"Ah," he said in satisfaction. His hunch had paid off. She was right on time. "Hi," he said when she came near.

Her head jerked up. One hand flew to her throat. For a split second she looked like a frightened deer caught in car headlights, then all signs of expression disappeared behind the heavy mask of makeup she wore.

"Oh, it's you," she said. "The deputy."

"Zack Dalton," he reminded her. "The cousin." He shot her a questioning glance, wondering if she would tell him her name or call for the security guards.

She hesitated, then spoke firmly, as if making up her mind it was okay to share the information. "My name is Hannah Carrington. I'm called Honey."

"Honey," he repeated, keeping his tone neutral. "Are you ready for supper? I'm starved."

"Are you joining me?" she asked with a certain wry amusement he found encouraging. Her lips, when she smiled, were delectable, like ripe cherries.

He grinned. "Yes, if you don't mind. My treat. I cashed in the quarters, so I'm flush. I, uh, also have an idea I'd like to discuss with you."

Once again seated in the coffee shop, he studied his companion while she glanced over the menu. Her absurd eyelashes cast long shadows over her rouged cheeks. He wondered how Uncle Nick would react to this "painted" woman.

Humor mingled with worry. The soft, full mouth with its sweet sensitivity belied the toughness implied by the makeup and costume. Which one was the true Honey Carrington?

His curiosity was piqued by the contradictions. Even if she wasn't Tink, he wanted to know more about this woman of unexpected depth and mystery.

Depth and mystery? He shook his head at his musings. Except for the scar, he really didn't know a solid fact about her, other than what she said.

After they'd ordered, he inhaled deeply, then began his argument to persuade her to return home with him. "I think I told you my uncle Nick had a heart attack recently?"

"Yes. That's why you're looking for his daughter."

"Right. I think you could be her." He held up a hand to forestall denials. "You have the scar. Both your parents are dead. You were raised by someone claiming to be a relative. What if she wasn't your aunt? What if you were taken from your mother's side and sold on the baby black market?"

"That's…that's ridiculous."

But she no longer sounded so certain, he noted. "So maybe something went wrong, and you didn't end up at the place you were supposed to go. Maybe the kidnapper needed to lie low and deposited you with a relative or girlfriend for safekeeping, but never came back. Where were you born?"

"California," she said, then glared at him for slipping the question in when she wasn't expecting it.

"You're sure of that?"

She lifted those fake eyelashes enough to stare at him in confusion. Her eyes were blue, light blue with silvery flecks. His heart upped its beat. Tink had had blue eyes.

"My aunt," she began in a low voice, then paused. "My aunt had to get a birth certificate for me when I went to school. It was certified by a sworn statement from her. She said I was born at home, with a midwife, instead of a doctor. Apparently the birth wasn't registered at the time.''

A shot of excitement zinged along Zack's nerves. The lack of a usual birth certificate clenched the matter as far as he was concerned. ''You have to come to the ranch and talk to Uncle Nick. I'll pay you. Five hundred dollars, free and clear, for two weeks of your time. You'll have room and board, of course.''

He couldn't tell anything from her silence.

''Look, it may not come to anything, but if there's a chance you're Tink, we have to take it. Uncle Nick might not survive another heart attack. If you are his daughter, wouldn't you want to know?''

The lush mouth trembled for just a second before she crimped her lips firmly against each other. ''Yes,'' she said in an almost inaudible voice. ''I'd want to know.''

He considered his anemic savings. ''Today's August the sixth. I'll give you a thousand if you'll stay the rest of the month.''

''I don't want your money,'' she told him seriously. ''Tink is your cousin's name?''

''Theresa. She insisted on Tinker Bell, so we started calling her Tink for short. It stuck.''

''You remember her?''

''Sure. I was around eight when she disappeared.''

Honey nodded and bent her head to study the table as if she might actually be considering his proposition.

Zack waited for her to think it through. While he had his own doubts about bringing a strange woman home, this was for Uncle Nick. He couldn't ignore the opportunity fate had thrown his way.

He saw her chest rise and fall. Bleakness darkened her eyes, then she said softly, "All right. I'll go with you. To Idaho, right?"

"Yes." He hooked an arm over the back of the chair and sighed in relief, unaware of the tension until that moment. "It isn't the end of the world," he assured her when she looked so oddly woebegone, or was it worried? Curiosity got the best of him. "Why have you decided to go?"

"I hate working in the casino."

The emotion underlying the statement spoke of truth. He wondered what he would have done if she'd refused. He could hardly kidnap her.

He smiled. He didn't have to worry about the next step now that she'd agreed with his plan. "What kind of notice do you need to give the casino?"

"Thirty minutes," she said with a cynicism touched with some other emotion he couldn't name. "People come and go at the drop of a hat here."

"Great. Can you be ready to leave at six in the morning?" At her startled glance, he said, "Okay, seven. Can you be ready by then? Where shall I pick you up?"

"I'll meet you in the lobby here. At six." She dropped her hands into her lap so the waitress could place her order on the table. "I'll need the address and phone number of the ranch. So I can tell my aunt,'' she added as if he'd questioned the need to know.

''No problem.'' He gave her the information. Picking up his hamburger, he bit into it hungrily. Lady Luck had finally smiled on him.

If this woman really was his long-lost cousin, Uncle Nick would be in high alt, as the old man liked to say.

But what if she wasn't? What if she was playing some game with them, hoping to cash in somehow? Huh, she'd refused the money he'd offered, so what could she want? And he'd been doing all the pursuing, so it was unlikely she'd planned it all. And let's face it, con artists weren't likely to target Idaho ranchers or deputy sheriffs!

He weighed the evidence. She had the scar, her parents were gone, her birth certificate was questionable, so there was the possibility that she was legitimate. For Uncle Nick's sake, he had to take that chance.

At five-thirty on Sunday morning, Honey left all her worldly possessions, which were crammed into two suitcases and one duffel, behind the supervisor's desk in the office that adjoined the employee lounge. No one was in at the moment, since it wasn't time for a shift change.

She didn't want any of her co-workers to spot her, dressed as she was in baggy pants, a tank top and a long-sleeved shirt, her hair hidden under a baseball cap with a skimpy dark-haired fake ponytail attached. She thought she looked enough like a boy to pass a casual glance, but she wasn't sure about a direct perusal from those who knew her.

Keeping her head low, she left the lounge and hurried to the elevators. At Zack's room, she slipped a note under the door.

It opened at once. "What is it?" he asked.

Startled, she could only stare up at him for a second, then she ducked her head. "I was told to deliver a message to this room, sir," she said in a deeper tone than her normal one. She gestured toward the letter.

"Wait," he ordered.

She froze in place.

He picked the letter up, tore open the envelope and read it, a suspicious frown on his face. Finished, he handed her two casino tokens worth a dollar each.

"No reply," he said, and closed the door.

She let her breath out slowly, then returned to the elevator. After leaving her employee badge and a note telling her supervisor she had to leave town due to a family emergency, she carried her luggage to the service door.

Zack appeared right on time. "Where is she?" he asked.

"I'm to take you to her," Honey told him. She pulled her baseball cap a little lower when he tilted his head and tried to study her face.

"Uh, this is her luggage," she added.

He nodded, hoisted the duffel and left her to deal with the two bags. She followed at his heels, taking longer steps in an insouciant and masculine—she hoped—manner.

They stored the bags in the back of a black SUV. She climbed in the passenger side, fastened her seat belt and slipped on sunglasses. She noted the protective bullet-proof glass and chain-link-type divider between the front and back seats. For a second she wondered if he would order her into the rear of the vehicle, where prisoners rode.

The deputy got in, started the engine, then eased into the sparse traffic along the strip.

Honey breathed a sigh of relief. Surely no one would expect her to leave Vegas in a vehicle emblazoned with the badge of a sheriff's department on its sides.

"Okay, where is she?" Zack demanded.

"Here," she said. She removed the sunglasses.

Zack stopped at the red light and turned to his passenger. The youngster he'd taken for a boy gave him a defiant grin.

The silvery-blue eyes met his. The lashes and eyebrows were golden brown. A tiny mole dotted the corner of her mouth, which was totally bare of makeup, as was the rest of her face. She looked fresh and young and entirely foreign to the waitress from the casino.

"What's going on?" he asked, feeling he'd been set up.

"Nothing," she said innocently.

Too innocently. He knew a scam when he saw one. "That getup is certainly different from your usual."

"I had to wear the casino costume. It was part of the job. Now I can dress in my own clothes."

The light turned and he drove on. "Those are your usual clothes? Tell me another one before that one gets cold."

Fury washed over him, but he wasn't usually a hot-tempered person. An effective cop had to consider the facts from a cool distance. He reached a logical conclusion.

They were on the highway now. The Sunday-morning traffic was heavier as people went to work in the resort town. He pulled off the road onto the shoulder just before an exit ramp and stopped. With the engine idling, he said, "What are you running away from?"

He had to give her credit for control. Her clasped hands tightened slightly, but that was her only reaction.

"I'm not," she said.

"Okay. *Who* are you running from?"

"No one."

"Either tell me, or I'll put you out right here and you can walk back to the casino."

The hands tightened again, then relaxed. "I don't know what you're talking about. We made a deal— the rest of the month at your uncle's ranch. That's what you said."

He locked eyes with her. If it hadn't been for that ever-so-slight tremor in the luscious mouth, he would have called off the whole thing. However, he felt a warning was called for. "If you try to bring any harm to my family, I'll ship you out so fast your head will spin."

"How could I do that? I don't even know them." She glared at him. "If you've changed your mind, the least you can do is take me back to my apartment before my landlady finds the note telling her I'm gone."

"You don't plan on coming back here?"

"It's a big world. I've only seen California and Nevada so far…and maybe Idaho if what you say is true."

This hard-edged, fresh-faced person was certainly at odds with the heavily made-up waitress who'd been concerned about him last night. More contradictions.

He put the police SUV in gear and headed north once more. Home was a sixteen-hour journey away. He planned to make it before midnight.

Out of the frying pan and into the fire.

Honey mocked her morbid thoughts as the miles peeled away under the tires. Other drivers, upon realizing the SUV was a sheriff's vehicle, slowed noticeably. It was evident they weren't sure of the authority of an out-of-state cop, but they weren't going to take any chances.

At midmorning they stopped for gas and picked up coffee and rolls at a fast-food drive-through. She watched the passing scenery, fascinated with the desert and colorful mountains.

When she asked about their travel plans, he told her they would follow Highway 93 to Twin Falls, pick up I-84 until they reached Boise, switch to state roads 55 and 95, then the county roads, which would take them to the ranch. He handed her a map from the door pocket.

Curious, she asked questions about the remote ranch. He answered each of them, painting an idealistic picture of his life with a stern but loving uncle and cousins galore. By the time she ran out of questions and his replies were growing shorter, she was filled with an envy that fueled the loneliness she felt as she traveled with the handsome deputy into the unknown.

For the rest of the day, she traced their route on the map as they drove north. They pulled into truck stops for gas and meals, first lunch, then dinner. As time passed, she couldn't help but feel she was on some grand adventure that would take her to…where?

Glancing at her companion, a tremor rippled through her like the warning quiver of an earthquake ready to roar up from the bowels of the earth. His perusal said he didn't quite trust her. She didn't blame him.

She fought a guilty conscience for taking advantage of his offer, knowing she wasn't the cousin he sought. However, she had to protect her brother, and that surely outweighed Zack's concern for his uncle. Didn't it? Anyway, he was the one who'd insisted she come with him, and truly she didn't mean the Daltons any harm.

While he drove, she studied him covertly. He was an attractive man. He wore no ring and had mentioned no wife in his list of family members, so she assumed he wasn't attached. If circumstances had been different, they might have met, fallen in love, even married.

Ah, she'd always been a romantic. A sigh, filled with sadness she couldn't quite fathom, worked its way out of her. At his quick look, she managed a smile.

Life was what it was, she reminded herself sharply. All the wishing and hoping and dreaming she'd ever done had never changed her fate, not one iota.

As the day grew longer, she became weary. She'd had no sleep the previous night due to her preparations for leaving. Her head dropped forward, startling her as she drifted into sleep. At last she asked, "Are we going to travel all night?"

"We'll stop at the next town if you're tired."

"How far are we from the ranch?"

"Four or five hours."

"I can make it. Are we in Idaho yet?"

"Just about."

She fell silent as tension crept up her neck. Whatever happened, she was committed to this course. For a moment she felt the way she had the day the social worker left her and Adam at her aunt's house, only this time she didn't have her brother's hand to cling to. She exhaled shakily. She was really, truly on her own.

Darkness closed around them. She glimpsed the sign that welcomed them to Idaho as it flashed past. At one point she heard his voice, but the words didn't register. "What?"

"You can let the seat back a little," he said more loudly. "The barrier keeps it from going very far."

She did so. The act was merely a blink on her consciousness, then it was gone.

Sometime later she was woken by a curse. She grasped warm flesh and felt the contraction in his thigh muscles as he braked, then the wild skid of the SUV as it swung in an arc. The rear end slid past the front and they came to an abrupt halt facing back the way they had come.

"What is it?" she asked, releasing her hold on him.

His snort was sardonic. "There's water across the road. Sit tight." He removed his shoes and socks, got out and checked the depth of the water.

Cold air swirled into the warm vehicle. Rain splattered in waves across it. She shivered and pulled her shirt closer around her. August in Idaho was definitely cooler than in Las Vegas.

The deputy returned, letting in another blast of chilly air. She looked around. There wasn't a house or building in sight, not even a distant light to indicate civilization.

Hail suddenly hit the windshield. "It's cold," she said. She was shivering.

"Yeah. We're caught in a freak storm. We're stuck until the water goes down."

Her escort dried his feet on a handkerchief, put on his shoes and socks, then restarted the SUV. He parked off road at a wide point that looked out on a shallow valley and a long range of mountains. The landscape all around them was lit by flashes of lightning.

She could detect evergreen trees and the ever-present desert sage. Along the edge of the road, Russian thistle and wallflowers formed soft mounds that constantly changed their shapes in the brisk wind. She shivered as if someone was walking on her grave.

"What do you mean, stuck?" she finally asked.

"As in, we can't go on."

"Well, let's go back," she said, wary of the storm and the dark.

"Where?" His tone was sardonic.

"The last town. We can stay in a motel until the storm is past."

He shook his head. "Sorry, but the last town was a hole in the wall with one quick-stop market-gas station combo, which, I might add, wasn't open."

"No motel?" she asked. Something akin to panic shot through her. She forced herself to stillness.

"Nothing." He slammed his fist on the steering wheel, the perfect picture of male irritation.

After a couple of minutes of silence, she dared ask, "What now?" The fact that not one car was visible in any direction wasn't lost on her.

"There's a town fifteen or twenty miles down the

road. That's a far piece to walk for help, even if we got across the flood over the road.'' He glanced at her. ''The current is swift, but I could probably make it.''

The thought of being left behind caused the near-panic to stir painfully. ''Maybe the water will subside soon.''

''Probably not before morning.''

He picked up the handset of a police scanner, his manner resigned but not particularly worried. All she heard was the crackle of static with a sharper crack at each flash of lightning on the horizon as he turned the dial. He tried calling several times, but got no answer.

When the lightning hit close, he turned the radio off. ''Too dangerous in this storm,'' he muttered.

''I have my cell phone.'' She got it out of her bag. When she tried to reach an operator in order to locate a nearby town and, she hoped, a place to stay, she got mostly static and faintly heard a recording that told her she was out of range. ''Out of range.''

He didn't appear surprised. ''Yeah. There's nothing open now, anyway.'' He yawned and stretched. ''We'll have to wait it out. Luckily the land drains fast. I have a sleeping bag.''

With that enigmatic statement, he got out, opened the rear door and climbed in. He laid the rear seats flat and spread a puffy bag over the cargo space.

''I can move our luggage so you can curl up back here and sleep,'' he told her.

Silently she watched while he stacked her three bags and one other against the back of the front seat.

"Sorry, no pillows," he said. He twisted and looked at her. "Your bed's ready."

The cold was getting to her now, and shivers racked her. "Where are you going to sleep?"

"In the front seat."

She immediately saw that this wasn't fair. "You're taller than I am. You take the back and I'll stay in the front."

He yanked a heavy parka from his bag and pulled it on. "I want to keep an eye on things. Excuse me," he said, then headed into the trees with a flashlight.

When he returned, he handed the light to her, got inside and slammed the door. She sat there for a minute, then also headed for the trees.

The rain had lightened to a fine mist, but the wind was still fierce. Upon returning, she hesitated, then climbed into the back of the vehicle since he already had his legs stretched along the bench-type front seat.

Even with the sleeping bag, she was aware of the cold seeping into the truck now that the engine was no longer supplying them with heat. The wind rocked the SUV like a dog shaking a bone as it moaned through sparse trees, across the road and over the ledge overlooking the valley. Other than the wind, no sounds disturbed the night.

She wondered where her brother was and if he was safe in bed somewhere. She thought of her aunt, who hadn't wanted two extra children to raise, and her cousin, who had tormented her until Adam bloodied his nose one day. She remembered her mother, who used to sing her to sleep with soft lullabies and old church songs.

Tears pushed upward from that deep place where she'd buried all painful memories. She couldn't afford to think of home or family or the things she didn't have.

Instead, she gazed at the night sky as the storm passed, heading east across the high desert, which appeared desolate to her eyes. A person could die out here and no one would know. Adam might never find out what had happened—

Stop it! There was no use in growing morbid. So she felt lonelier than a howling coyote, so what? There were worse things—like being dead.

She forced her eyes closed. Her muscles ached from fatigue, and her feet were slowly turning to ice. She slept, but she woke up cold and whimpering in fear.

"Honey? Wake up. You're dreaming," an oddly familiar voice told her.

"A nightmare," she said in a hoarse whisper. "I was in the Arctic or somewhere. It was so cold. I thought I was freezing. My feet still feel like ice cubes," she said, putting a humorous twist to the words.

"Do you have a coat or something?"

She retrieved her old trench coat from her duffel and slipped it on, then pulled the sleeping bag up to her neck.

"Hand me my bag, will you?" he requested. "I can't sleep without a pillow."

She heard the chain divider rattle, then in the dim light of a pale moon she saw he'd let one side down. She handed his nylon bag to him. He squashed it until he was satisfied with its shape, then snuggled down.

Zack was aware of his passenger's unease and wariness. He knew fear could produce a chill and regretted the trip had turned into more of an adventure than he'd expected. "I'll warm the truck."

He cranked the engine and turned the air vents so the warm air would circulate into the back. He flicked on the radio and ran the tuner through the channels. Nothing.

"Has the water gone down?" she asked.

"Not yet."

After a few minutes he heard her sigh and sensed the relaxing in her vigil. She was asleep.

A spark shot through him, causing heat to spear through his groin. It had been a while since he'd slept with a woman in a space this small. Not that they were actually sleeping together in a physical sense. But he was aware of her.

Work had kept him busy. Summers were harried because of tourists getting themselves into some jam or another. Winter heralded hunters who got themselves lost. A spring blizzard had brought its own woes. He hadn't thought about dating in months, much less more interesting things.

So here he was, sleeping in the truck with a woman he'd found in the casino capital of the world, bringing her home to possibly become part of his family. He was worried about that. He didn't want Uncle Nick to be hurt in case they were wrong to trust her.

He went over the facts. Gone was the shapely, thickly painted waitress. In her place was a slender female who had actually fooled him into thinking she was a boy. Well, only for a short time. Without makeup, she was prettier and softer-looking.

That was what bothered him. There was something vulnerable about her, as if she needed lots of TLC.

Huh, he'd always been a sucker for every lost dog or cat to cross his path.

Pushing his lumpy pillow against the door for a back rest, he stared into the night. From over the far peaks, he heard the rumble of the passing storm. He hoped it wouldn't rain anymore so they could get on their way at the crack of dawn.

Honey stirred and gave a slight sound in her sleep. A bolt of hunger went through him like the heat lightning on the eastern horizon. Now he was more than hot. He was rock-hard and tense with needs that weren't going to be met in the near future.

Damnation, she might be his cousin, he reminded his libido. Since he hadn't grown up with her, it would be hard to think of her as such if that turned out to be the case.

If not, there were other possibilities.

Waitress, tomboy, lover. There was a certain irony in the chain of thought, but at the present he didn't find it humorous. Too much need raged through him.

From the other side of the seat, she moved again,

pushing the sleeping bag aside as she grew warm. He cut the engine. The silence closed around them. He heard her sigh.

An electrical current shot through every nerve in his body. The dark felt sweetly intimate as he listened to the wind outside and the quiet sound of her breathing. If he woke her now, who would she be? Waitress? Cousin? Tomboy? Or lover?

None of the above, he mocked the thought.

It was his last thought before he fell asleep, the odd bliss of some forgotten happiness filling his dreams.

Chapter Three

Honey awoke with a groan. Her companion chuckled. She realized his stirring had disturbed her.

"The truck makes for an uncomfortable bed," he mentioned cheerfully. "Even with carpet and a sleeping bag."

"I noticed." She peered at the faint light in the sky behind the hills. "What time is it?"

"Late. A little after five," he added when she frowned at him. "I want to get home before noon."

"Why?"

"Work," he explained patiently. "I have to take you to the ranch, then head back to town."

"You wouldn't be going to the ranch if it weren't for me, would you?"

"That's right."

"You don't live there with your uncle?"

"Not all the time. I have a room in town."

Combing her fingers through her hair, she watched him get out and walk to the rear of the SUV.

"Sorry about the cold," he said, opening the rear door. He removed, then set up a little camping stove, poured water from a plastic jug and put it on to boil.

"Tea or coffee?" he called.

"Coffee."

"Sugar? Powdered milk?"

"One sugar, please." She cautiously pushed the covers down, creeping tentatively from the warmth of the sleeping bag. The temperature felt frigid to her.

"I'll bring it to you."

When he handed her the cup, she was almost too surprised to thank him. "It's nice to be waited on."

"Enjoy it while you can. It isn't my usual style."

She sipped the hot brew while he checked the road and declared it safe. The water was no more than six inches deep now. She retrieved her travel kit, freshened up, then paid a visit to the other side of the trees.

"You seem to think of everything—sleeping bag, stove, coffee, tea," she said as they finished the last of the coffee, both of them in the front seat again.

"A person would be foolish to live in the mountains and not be prepared to wait out a storm."

"Do you get lots of snow in Idaho?"

He grinned in that special way he had—rather humorous, more than a little sexy and definitely intriguing. It was his smile that had first suggested she could trust him. He'd rewarded her faith by being a perfect gentleman last night.

"Not as much as some places, but enough. Put that parka on. It's about thirty-six degrees this morning," he told her. "I don't want you catching a chill before I get you to the ranch. My gear doesn't extend to nursing facilities."

She sighed raggedly, grateful her trust hadn't been misplaced. There were so few people she dared put her confidence in these days. This man was very... nurturing.

She considered the descriptive word and, while she sensed there was more, much more, to the handsome deputy, it was a reasonable assessment of him.

"Ready?" he asked.

She nodded and noticed his glance at her hair. Since she didn't have to hide it under a cap, she'd left it down around her shoulders.

"You look very different from your casino appearance."

Lifting her chin, she returned his cool appraisal. "That was for work."

"Or to hide your identity from someone?"

Her heart lurched at his correct assessment. She started to reply, then thought better of it. When unsure of what to say, it was better to be silent. He studied her briefly, then started the truck and drove onto the pavement. Almost three hours later, they arrived at a small lake formed by a dam. A community nestled close by. She opened the map of the state and asked where they were.

"Lost Valley. The town serves the ranchers and the tourists taking the scenic route on their way to Yellowstone or the Tetons or, heading west, those going to Hells Canyon in the summer."

In the winter, she imagined, the place must be like a deep freeze. She mused on what it would be like, being snowed in for days on end. Her gaze was drawn to Zack, and her heart gave another of those odd lurches.

"Dalton," she said suddenly. "Wasn't there a gang by that name in the Wild West days?"

"Yeah. There's a connection, but we're descended from the branch that had the good guys."

His grin was infectious. Smiling, she studied the map again and then the peaks around them when they topped a hill west of the valley.

From this vantage point, she could see all the way down to Lost Valley and the tiny town of the same name tucked in close to the reservoir. The valley was 5000 feet high, according to the map. He-Devil Mountain to the north was 9393 feet high. They were someplace between the two and still climbing.

"We're nearly home," he told her.

She gazed all around the panoramic scene of peaceful valley and majestic peaks, the lake and evergreen trees. "It's beautiful here," she said. "The most beautiful place I've ever seen."

He gave her a skeptical glance.

"Well, I've only been in Southern California and then Nevada, actually only in Las Vegas, until yesterday," she admitted. "But I've always been fascinated by mountains and how they formed, the vast upheavals of the earth and the forces of nature and all that."

"Yeah, it's fascinating," he agreed.

She couldn't tell if he was being sarcastic or sincere. Keeping her thoughts to herself, she picked out more odd names on the map. There was a She-Devil Mountain, the mate to He-Devil, she decided, smiling.

"What's funny?" he asked.

"The names. Seven Devils Mountains. He-Devil. She-Devil. Are there others?"

"There's one called the Devil's Tooth. Another is Mount Ogre. Mmm, the Tower of Babel, Mount Baal, the Goblin. Those are the official seven. On the ranch, we have an escarpment with a flat boulder on it that we named the Devil's Dining Room."

"Does your Uncle Nick live there alone?"

"No. My twin brothers live on the ranch. My cousins live in Boise but visit often."

"How many cousins did you say you have?"

"Three."

A frisson swept along Honey's scalp. Zack, his two brothers, the three cousins and Uncle Nick. That made seven. She inhaled sharply as her imagination leaped from the seven Daltons to the Seven Devils Mountains.

As if reading her thoughts, he said, "No, the mountains weren't named in honor of my family."

Looking at his devilish grin, she wondered about that.

Honey realized she would never find her way back to town as they wound around hills and through canyons. At last they crossed a wooden bridge over a dry creek, and the land opened into a flat valley ringed by tree-covered ridges.

Nestled on a rise, protected in a curving sweep of pine trees, was a stone and split-log ranch house. "Rambling" described it perfectly. Wings spread out to each side of the central structure, which had a porch across its face.

"Home," Zack said. "There's Uncle Nick."

An older man came out onto the porch. His hair was white and lay in an attractive wave sweeping back from his forehead just like his nephew's. His face was tanned and lined. A tall man, as tall as Zack, his rangy frame retained the lanky appearance of youth. She estimated his age to be late sixties, early seventies.

"What happened to your parents?" she asked.

"They died when we were young."

"How?"

"My father and mother, plus my dad's twin brother and his girlfriend, came home one year to visit, bringing us kids with them. They went out on the town one night. There was an avalanche and they never made it back. Since Uncle Nick was the only kin, he and Aunt Milly were saddled with six additional kids to raise."

"Aunt Milly was the one who died in the accident? It was her little girl who was kidnapped?"

"Yes."

Honey considered the events that had occurred in his family. Like her, Zack was an orphan who had been taken in by a relative. She felt a bond with him, one of tragedy.

"I'm sorry about your parents and the others," she said a bit stiffly, but sincerely.

"It was a long time ago."

"How old were you?"

"Seven. I don't remember much about it."

The bleakness of his tone belied that. She started to ask him where he'd lived prior to coming to the ranch, but was forestalled when he parked and leaped out of the truck.

"Wait here," he said, and slammed the door.

Her heart set up a cacophony as she watched him greet his uncle, then gesture toward the truck as he talked. The uncle stared at her. They talked some more. Finally Zack waved for her to join them.

Reluctantly she did so, then waited for the older man to denounce her as a liar and opportunist. He studied her, his eyes as blue as Zack's, but shrewd with age. When he reached out and lifted her chin, she met his eyes.

He smiled. "So you think you might be Tink?"

She shook her head. "Your nephew thinks so. I'm Hannah Carrington. Everyone calls me Honey."

"Zack told me about your circumstances," the uncle said thoughtfully.

Her heart did a flip until she realized Zack couldn't possibly know her real circumstances.

"Your parents are gone and you've lived with an aunt since you were three or thereabouts?" the old man added.

"Yes, that's right."

"There was a question about your birth certificate?"

"I'm sure that's just one of those odd coincidences that occurs at times." She tried to sound honest and yet unsure enough to maintain a question about her birth.

He patted her cheek, something she wouldn't have normally appreciated, but that seemed comforting coming from this kindly old gentleman. Like the nephew, he was a caring person.

"I'm glad you're here," he said in simple welcome. "Show her to the rose room, Zack. I'll put lunch on the table."

"Are you supposed to be up and cooking?" Zack asked.

"Don't fuss," the old man said amiably. "The doc said I have to walk an hour every day. I figure if I can walk, I can cook and clean up the house a little."

Honey saw Zack's chest rise and fall in an exasperated breath, but he said nothing as his uncle went inside.

"It's hard to keep help out here," Zack said to her, heading for the SUV. "It's too far from town. We've had about a dozen housekeepers over the years. They stay six months, maybe a year, then the isolation gets to them.''

He handed her the duffel, tucked his nylon bag under one arm, then lifted out her two heavy suitcases.

Clenching a hand into a fist in a sudden spasm of panic, she followed him inside. Her feet seemed to be coated in lead as they entered the rustic dwelling.

They passed through a comfortably furnished living room and turned right into a hallway. He guided her past two open bedroom doors and went into a third one, the last in this wing of the house.

''This is lovely,'' she said, feeling very much the deceptive interloper.

The room was twice as big as the other bedrooms they'd passed. It ran the depth of the wing and had a large sitting area that faced the front yard. A door opened onto a path from that side.

The windows flanking the bed looked out on a small backyard edged by towering trees that grew up a steep ridge, where a forest of firs and pines spread outward and upward over the land.

Zack paused. He looked at the bed, then back to her. His eyes seemed to darken. She felt some secret inner part of her expand painfully, pushing on her lungs so she couldn't breathe all of a sudden. She couldn't look away as tension arced between them.

Turning abruptly, he placed her bags on the floor in front of a double set of matching doors. He opened those to disclose a spacious closet. ''The bathroom is next door. The dining room is on the other side of the kitchen. Can you be ready to eat in five minutes?''

She nodded.

After he left, her nerves calmed slightly. She slowly pivoted, taking in the wallpaper with the big pink roses and soft green leaves, the sparkling white beadboard that formed the wainscoting and the sturdy oak furniture. A lacy white bedspread interspersed with pink roses covered pale-green sheets on the queen-size bed.

The soft-rose decor wasn't the sort a household of bachelors would choose. She wondered what woman had picked it out and felt a strange emotion stir in her breast. It took a moment, but she finally recognized it as envy.

Some girl had been lucky to have this room, she thought, fighting the harsh sting of longing as she went to the bathroom and freshened up before facing Zack and his uncle again. That girl had been cherished.

Inhaling carefully, she dried her face, combed her hair and returned to the middle of the house. Four men were busy putting food on the table.

She stopped, her mouth dry, feeling like a rabbit who'd stumbled into a den of wolves. Her feet stuck to the floor.

One of the men spotted her. ''Hi. Come on in. We only look dangerous, but no one bites. Uncle Nick lost his teeth years ago, and we're not allowed to devour pretty women.''

''I have all my own teeth,'' Uncle Nick corrected his nephew balefully, then smiled at her, showing off what appeared to be a perfectly good set of natural teeth.

She managed a return smile of sorts.

Zack placed a bowl of mashed potatoes on the table. "Sit," he said unceremoniously and held a chair for her. "This is Honey Carrington," he said as if it was perfectly normal to show up with a strange woman in tow.

She sat and let out another careful breath. Zack took the chair beside her while the older man sat at the end of the table to her immediate right. The twins were opposite.

"I'm Trevor, the handsome twin," the first man who'd spoken informed her, his manner friendly and easy. "That's Travis. He's the quiet, ugly one."

"You look identical," she said, smiling at his joke.

Travis chuckled while his twin clutched his chest as if wounded. "I'd hoped you could tell the difference," Trevor said in complaint, then spoiled it with a grin.

"We'll have a blessing," Uncle Nick said.

Honey bowed her head when the men did. Uncle Nick thanked the Lord for bringing Honey to them and recounted other blessings. She felt such an impostor. A brief silence ensued, then the uncle said, "Amen."

"Potatoes?" Zack asked, handing her the bowl.

She took a small serving of each dish as it was passed. There were several to go along with the meat loaf, so her plate ended up filled to the edges. She gazed at it in dismay, not sure she could swallow. She choked down a bite of everything.

"You don't have to eat it all," Uncle Nick said kindly.

"Thank you. It's more than I realized. But everything is delicious," she quickly added in case she hurt the uncle's feelings with her lack of appetite.

"So, Zack says you may be our long-lost cousin," Trevor began after a brief silence. "Where did he find you?"

"In Vegas," Zack answered before she could. He smiled. "She brought me luck. She found a quarter I dropped. When I put it in the slot machine, I hit the jackpot for six hundred quarters." He turned to her. "I meant to give you a big tip."

Heat rose to her cheeks. "That's okay."

"A hundred and fifty dollars," Travis, the quiet twin, commented. "You were lucky."

"How much did you blow before you won?" the uncle asked shrewdly.

Zack grinned. "Twenty dollars."

"Huh," Uncle Nick said.

Honey wasn't sure if the older man disapproved of the gambling. When he turned his startling blue eyes on her, she felt like a kid called on the carpet.

"Honey and I are going to talk after we eat," he said. "Privately."

Her chest actually hurt as she thought of the deception she was perpetrating. Although she wasn't lying about her past, she'd cast enough doubt to leave the question of her origins open. She hadn't mentioned her brother at all.

A sigh worked its way out of her. She had to protect Adam. He was her first concern.

Unexpectedly Uncle Nick patted her hand. His wise gaze seemed to peer right into her soul. Instead of feeling cornered, she felt comforted, as if he knew her troubles.

"You're welcome in this house," he said.

"Thank you." Her voice trembled, a fact she couldn't conceal. Honestly. In another minute she would dissolve into tears and confess all. Would they throw her out? Or would they take her under their wing like some stray kitten?

"Were you in Vegas on vacation?" Travis wanted to know.

She glanced at Zack, then said truthfully, "I was working as a cocktail waitress."

"Ah," the other twin said as if that explained a lot. Not a smidgen of condemnation entered his gaze.

She couldn't stand it another second. Pushing her chair back, she stood abruptly. Four pairs of pure blue eyes stared up at her. "I…excuse me. I need to…to rest for a while."

Coward and liar that she was, she fled to the pretty bedroom, closed and locked the door behind her, then flung herself on the lace coverlet, tears she wouldn't let fall burning her eyes like hot coals. She'd never felt so miserable.

Zack shrugged when his brothers stared at him across the table. "Women," he said in answer to their unvoiced questions. He turned to his uncle. "What do you think?"

Uncle Nick buttered a roll before glancing his way. "I think she needs to rest just as she said. What time did you make her get on the road this morning?"

"Early," he admitted. Since he'd never been able to hide the truth from Uncle Nick, he told about the storm and having to spend the night in the truck.

"Ahh," drawled Trevor softly.

Zack glared at his brother. "She might be our cousin," he said by way of explaining their sleep had been of the most innocent variety.

"Maybe. Maybe not," Trevor said thoughtfully.

Zack kept his mouth shut and finished his meal. The abundant and simple food was delicious compared to the fast food he'd consumed on the road.

After he and Honey had made it into a small town that morning, he'd bought doughnuts, milk and coffee for them at the gas-station mart while they filled up. He hadn't thought to stop later for a more substantial breakfast.

"You want to talk to Honey now?" he asked Uncle Nick when the older man finished eating.

His uncle considered, then shook his head. "She might be asleep. I thought she looked tired."

"Yeah. We left early yesterday and she didn't get off work until two that morning. She didn't sleep much last night, either. Nightmares," he explained at his brothers' identical glances.

"What made you think she was our cousin?" Travis, the quiet twin, asked.

Zack told them about his winnings and the accident that had caused him to drop the bucket of quarters. He vaguely described Honey's outfit and how he'd just happened to notice the scar on her thigh. He didn't say they'd both been on their knees picking up quarters at the time, his nose no more than six inches from her...well, it wasn't necessary to go into fine detail.

"Oh, yeah, I've seen what those gals in Vegas wear," Trevor agreed.

"You've never even been there," Zack scoffed.

"I've seen movies," the twin asserted, looking wise.

Zack refrained from punching him out, then wondered why he was getting so hot under the collar. There was no reason for him to defend Honey.

"Let the girl alone," Uncle Nick said, putting an end to the conversation. "She's probably taking a nap. I'll talk to her later. Isn't it time you boys got to work?"

The twins took their plates to the kitchen and put them in the dishwasher, then departed for the stable. Zack yawned and thought about a snooze himself.

He helped his uncle clear the table and clean up the kitchen, then Uncle Nick went to his room and Zack sprawled on the leather sofa in the living room, which had once been the entire cabin, built more than 150 years ago.

The homestead had been added to over the years.

Uncle Nick had remodeled the east wing and added a master bedroom when he married. The west wing, where Honey was, had been constructed after the six cousins had arrived in order to accommodate the influx of growing children. Uncle Nick and his wife had never considered sending the five nephews and one niece to an orphanage.

His last thought was of the ranch and how nice it was to be home again. The rest of the world was okay for a visit, but this was home. He wondered if Honey would like it here.

Honey awoke with a little cry of fear. It was dark and she didn't know where she was. Instead of sitting up, she lay still and listened intently, then opened her eyes.

Only after she was sure no one was lurking nearby did she push herself to a sitting position. The room was in deep shadow, but she knew where she was now.

The Dalton ranch. Uncle Nick and the twins. Zack.

As information came flooding back to her consciousness, she wondered if her brother had found a safe haven and hoped he would send an e-mail or call soon. She'd sent him the phone number and address of the ranch.

Rising, she changed from the baggy boy's clothing to black cotton-knit slacks and a black top. She freshened up and went to the living room, where Uncle Nick was watching TV.

"Did you sleep?" he asked, giving her a kind smile.

"Yes." She glanced at a wall clock. It was almost seven. "I didn't realize how long until now."

"You needed the rest. Come sit a spell and we'll talk."

She recoiled from the idea of telling more lies, either outright or by hesitation and implication. However, there was no other choice. She sat in the corner of the sofa.

At the other end, a pillow still showed an imprint as if someone had been lying there. She instinctively knew it had been Zack. An unexpected warmth flowed over her and with it, a confidence in her decision to come north with him.

"Tell me about yourself," the old man invited.

"What would you like to know?"

"Anything you care to share."

"Well, my birth certificate shows I was born at home, near Bakersfield, California. My aunt said I was."

There, in the semidarkness, she told him of her early life, about her parents' deaths, her aunt and cousin, and what it had been like growing up an orphan. She didn't mention Adam, but still felt she might have told more than she meant to due to her host's gentle probing. He asked questions in a way that didn't seem like prying. His manner was kind and interested, as if she meant something as a person to him. At last she fell silent.

"Do you recall anything of your mother?"

She sorted through her memories. "Some. She used to sing to me. Sometimes, in dreams, I hear a woman's voice singing old songs. I think that was real."

"We had a housekeeper one time," he murmured. "She used to sing while she cooked, old spirituals we all loved. She stayed longer than any other help we ever had. Tink was three when she retired and moved to Texas."

Guilt stabbed Honey right in the chest. "Mr. Dalton, I don't really think I could be your daughter. I mean, I don't remember this place, not the mountains or house or…or anything. I don't feel that I belong here. I'm sorry."

"Everyone calls me Uncle Nick," he said. "You may as well, too. Don't worry about whether you belong or not. Sometimes a place can grow on you."

His eyes held a warm glow when he turned on a floor lamp beside his chair. She couldn't help but smile at him, although her composure was a bit shaky. Deception was a lot harder than she'd realized.

"The boys ate supper earlier," Uncle Nick continued. "There was a county meeting in town they had to attend."

She battled a brief depression. "I see."

"Zack went to town, but he's back now."

Her spirits lifted. "He's here? I thought he said something about having a room in town."

"I think he's afraid to leave you alone with me and the twins. We might be a dangerous bunch."

She smiled at his teasing. "I find all of you charming," she assured him.

"How did you get to Nevada?" he asked. "You said you hadn't been out of California until three months ago."

For a minute she couldn't decide how much of her life to disclose. Adam said to always tell as much of the truth as possible to avoid getting tripped up later.

"I was part of a dance company, one that folded," she quickly improvised. "I had to find another job right away, since my savings didn't stretch to idle living."

That much was true, but the history belonged to the first professional troupe she'd danced with.

"So working in the casino was a temporary thing while you looked for other work?" he questioned.

She could answer that without qualms. "Well, I hoped so. The competition for shows is tough in Vegas. After New York and Los Angeles, it's a prime location for dancers, singers and comedians."

"You must have been good to earn a position with a group from Los Angeles," he concluded. "How many were in your dance company?"

"Twelve to fifteen, according to who was injured or off on other things, such as getting married or having babies. Like opera singers and celebrities, we're scheduled for months, even years, in advance, so you have to work in your personal life where you can."

"Sounds busy."

"Yes, it was."

"Do you miss it?" he asked.

A feeling like homesickness came over her. She missed the dancing. Not the excitement of an opening or the applause of the crowd or even the other dancers, but the music, the movement itself. Those had given her the sense of freedom her soul had craved during those years growing up in her aunt's house. She stared at her clasped hands until the emotion dissolved.

"Some," she admitted.

A shadow crossed the window. She recognized Zack's rangy frame. He entered the front door, hung his hat and coat on a rack and greeted them.

"Another storm is brewing. It's getting cold out there," he said, pulling off his boots. He placed them neatly under the coatrack and padded over to the leather chair to the left of the sofa. "Did you sleep?"

"Yes, I did," she murmured.

He gestured toward the doorway. "I'm going to raid the kitchen. Have you eaten?"

"Not yet."

"Join me," he invited.

He led the way and handed her a plate, took one for himself, then removed leftovers from the refrigerator. He heated her stuff in the microwave first, then his. They sat at a smaller table in the kitchen.

"Did Uncle Nick grill you?" he asked.

She quickly swallowed the bite she'd taken. "Sort of. He's skillful at drawing a person out," she added tactfully.

Zack chuckled, an attractive sound in the quiet

kitchen. In the living room, the television added soft background noise to the ambiance of the house. She imagined Zack and his family gathered around the hearth, sharing their day and enjoying the safety from the cold outside.

"What?" he said suddenly.

She gazed at him. The question made no sense.

"You sighed," he said. "Are you bored here?"

"Oh, no," she assured him. "The mountains are lovely. And so is the house. And my bedroom."

He nodded. "It's my favorite place."

Curiosity overcame her manners. "You and your brothers, how come there aren't wives and children on the ranch? It seems the perfect spot to raise a family."

"It is." He studied her for a few seconds with those fathomless blue eyes. "So why are there only bachelors here? I guess we haven't met the right mates. Except for Travis. He's engaged. Actually, he was married once before, but his wife died in childbirth."

"How terrible. When did it happen?"

"A couple of years ago. It was pretty awful, but this spring he met someone, so it worked out for him. Alison's father is a politician and she's helping the new campaign manager settle in, so they don't have a lot of time together now. And she's getting things together for the wedding—which Travis is happy to leave up to her—and then moving here afterward."

"I see. Are any of your cousins married?"

"Not yet. Uncle Nick is getting worried. Seth is the

oldest at thirty-three. I turned thirty last month. When is your birthday?''

''This month, the twenty-fifth,'' she said without thinking.

''According to your aunt's sworn statement.''

''That's right.'' She lifted her chin and dared him to call it a lie.

''Tink will be twenty-six in September.''

''If she's still alive. I read that most kidnap victims, if not found within twenty-four hours, are usually…''

''Dead,'' he finished coolly when she couldn't say the word. ''That's true. It's something we've had to consider. However, a body was never found, so that's given us hope.''

''Yes, there is that.''

Zack watched Honey carefully, but he couldn't tell what was on her mind. One minute she seemed infinitely sad, the next, almost defiant, as if she dared him to question her.

She was one of those mysteries wrapped in an enigma and tied up in a question mark. A big question mark.

He studied her blond hair with the dark roots, the light blue of her eyes, the paleness of her skin. She wasn't the outdoors type, he surmised. Which meant she wasn't his type, either.

Not that he'd done so great with his first choice, who had been a local girl.

But his wife had to be at home in the mountains. They might have a house in town, but they'd spend a lot of time out on the ranch. They would ride and roam the hills....

He reversed the direction his thoughts had taken. He wasn't looking for a wife. No way.

Chapter Four

Zack escorted Honey to the living room when they finished their meal and joined Uncle Nick in watching his favorite shows, which were either news, nature documentaries or true-crime docudramas.

Honey excused herself before ten and went to her room. Zack inhaled deeply, acknowledging relief. She caused a tension in him that he didn't like, especially considering she might be a relative.

"Did you have a talk with Honey?" he asked his uncle.

"Mmm-hmm," Uncle Nick said, not taking his eyes from the screen, where a shadowy murderer lurked outside a house in a college neighborhood.

Zack curbed his impatience. "What did you think?"

The screen cut to a commercial. Uncle Nick looked at him as if he could see clear to his soul. "That you can relax. I don't think the girl is Tink."

Zack sat up straight. "What?"

"Her eyes are too light."

"Don't eyes change color as kids grow? Besides, Honey has the scar. And her eyes *are* blue, just not as dark as the rest of us. Besides, Seth's eyes are brown, so not all Daltons have blue eyes."

"Well, they mostly do," his uncle said, using his own brand of stubborn logic. "But you have a point about the scar. Her past is a bit of a mystery, too." He sighed. "I always thought I'd know my own daughter instantly, but I guess that was sentimental foolishness. I like this Honey Carrington. She's troubled about something, though."

Zack's heart upped its tempo as Uncle Nick confirmed his own gut feelings about their guest. "What? Did she tell you anything?"

"No. Perhaps you could sound her out. She might need help. Anyway, I'd feel better knowing you were keeping tabs on her while she's here. Take her sightseeing." He smiled innocently.

Zack saw right through his uncle's reasoning to the matchmaking hopes of the old man, who wanted every Dalton married and settled down before he kicked the bucket. However, Zack fully intended to keep an eye on the beautiful stranger he'd brought into their midst.

"Tell me what she said about herself. Let's see if it jibes with what she's told me," he requested.

Uncle Nick gave him the details of the discussion with their guest. Other than more info on the aunt and cousin and apparently a dancing career, it agreed with what she'd told him.

Honey retrieved her trench coat from her duffel. She'd rarely worn it—until hitting Idaho. Once it had had a zip-out lining, but that had been lost years ago. She pulled it on over the long-sleeved shirt and eased open the door to the outside.

The flagstone path meandered along the bedroom wing to the front porch. In the other direction, it turned the corner of the house, presumably leading to the backyard.

A cold west wind whipped around the eaves with a low keening sound. From someplace beyond the barns and stables, she heard the lowing of cattle and a whicker from a horse.

Crossing the narrow lawn and the road in front of the house, she went to the fence beside the stables. A horse rushed over and thrust its nose into her hand, demanding to be petted. She scratched its ears.

The animal blew softly against her neck, giving a contented sigh like that of a satisfied lover. Impulsively she hugged its neck and pressed her face into its rough mane as a sense of desolation swept over her.

Of necessity, she'd left her friends behind when she went into hiding. She felt small and unimportant in the grand scheme of things, alone in a world that cared nothing for human woes.

She wept silently and without tears for the father she'd never known, for a mother she vaguely recalled, for the brother who was only a shadow in her life, for a man she'd once thought she loved and who had deceived her.

The horse patiently accepted her outpouring of grief, and for a few terrible minutes, she gave in to emotion. Then the animal moved back enough to nudge her shoulder with its nose. Its eyes gleamed softly in the moonlight.

"It's okay," she murmured. "I'm okay now."

The horse gave a disbelieving snort, which made her smile. She pushed her hair behind her ears and headed for the house. A figure stepped off the front porch.

"Can't sleep?" Zack asked, joining her in the roadway between the stables and the house.

"No."

She fell into step beside him and they walked down the road toward the moon, which was a sliver of silver, cold, distant and magical, hanging over a mountain peak.

After a quarter of a mile, the road narrowed and stopped at a gate in the stock fence. "Where does it go?" she asked, pointing across the field. "To another house?"

"Sort of. It's a logging road into the mountains that connects to another ranch. Several trails join it, and one goes to the top of that ragged peak. People, mostly hikers and hunters, get lost up there, two or three each year.''

''Then you have to go find them?''

''Yes. We have a mounted search-and-rescue team who helps the sheriff's department when necessary.''

''I see.''

''You made a friend for life earlier. The mare loves to have her ears scratched.''

Honey hoped he hadn't seen her clinging to the animal as if it was her last hope in the world. ''What's her name?''

''Johnny's Girl. Her sire was a quarter horse named Johnny. Her dam was Frankie.''

''Frankie and Johnny,'' Honey repeated. ''I hope their romance ended better than the one in the song.''

His chuckle was low and deep, a musical fugue with the night wind that hummed down off the ridge, stirring her hair and blowing the lightweight knit slacks against her.

She shivered and hugged her coat tightly around her.

''You're cold,'' Zack noted. ''Let's go back. I'll take you for a tour of the place in the morning. Do you ride?''

''No.''

''It's a matter of balance and knowing when to hang on. With your agility, you'll catch on in no time.''

''How do you know I'm agile?''

''The way you move. Uncle Nick said you'd been

a dancer. I might have seen you. Were you one of the showgirls in the casino?''

''No. The dance company put on special performances. Sometimes we did parodies of *Swan Lake* and other famous ballets. The audiences loved those. We performed dances from different countries, such as the Irish clog and Spanish flamenco and—''

She stopped abruptly as she realized her enthusiasm was running away with her tongue. She had to be on guard about her past. The truth, but only so much of it, she reminded herself harshly.

''Sounds interesting. You must miss it.''

''Some, but it was a hard life.'' She shrugged to show it didn't matter.

''So is ranching, but I wouldn't trade it for anything.''

''You're a deputy sheriff.''

''Well, I like that, too, especially since it pays the bills and lets me dabble around with horse breeding and trading without having to live on the income. I want to develop a line of champion cutting horses.''

Again his chuckle wafted over her, confident of his chosen path and his place in the world. She envied him that.

They arrived at the house. He led the way to her bedroom door. When he opened it and she stepped inside, he followed.

''Will you be up by eight?'' he asked. ''I thought we'd take the tour at that time. I have to report in at the office by twelve. I'll be working second shift, from noon until ten, the rest of this week.''

''You don't have to show me around.''

''Uncle Nick told me to,'' he said. His smile flashed quick and bright at her.

She smiled, too. She'd already ascertained that one did as Uncle Nick said. ''Then yes, eight is fine.''

He started for the hall door, then paused, his eyes dark in the dim glow coming from a night-light in the bathroom. A tremor swept over her as she felt his brief but intense scrutiny almost as a tactile sensation.

She wondered what his thoughts were…what he thought of her as a person…as a woman…

The longing hit her. She didn't know what she wanted, but it was acute and reached into her soul.

He brought his hand up and touched her cheek with one finger.

Moving back, she lifted her chin as he dropped his hand and studied her. She had to stop these ridiculous yearnings.

Finally he spoke. ''There's something soft and kind of lost about you. Uncle Nick has a tender heart for orphans.''

''What about you?'' she heard herself say, then was immediately appalled.

What was the matter with her tonight? Her emotions and tongue seemed on a roller coaster that was on the brink of disaster. Where was her discipline? Her control?

''I've been known to take in a stray or two,'' he

admitted in a gruff tone. "But I've been in law enforcement long · enough to be wary. I brought you home to my family. I hope that wasn't a mistake."

"You don't have to worry," she informed him coolly. "I've told you the truth about myself."

Most of the truth. She would tell Uncle Nick as much as she thought was safe, she decided, if she had to leave before the month was over. He deserved that from her.

Zack's expression changed slightly. His eyes went to her lips. He touched one corner of her mouth. "It's real," he said. "I'd wondered about the beauty mark. You made it darker before, but it's there."

The tiny mole burned like fire.

"It's hard to tell what's real and what isn't about you," he continued, questions in his eyes. "Maybe I'll find out during the coming month."

She pushed his hand away. "Don't count on it. I'm here for your uncle, because I felt sorry for him and his loss." She swallowed as the truth crowded to the tip of her tongue. "And because I was tired," she added candidly. "I didn't like working in the casino, but there were no other openings at the time."

"Until I came along. Did men bother you?"

"Not much. Security is tight. You probably noticed."

He gave her a wry grimace. "I did. I also noticed you."

"The scar," she corrected.

"The shape of your legs and the way they come

down to a V at your ankles, the slenderness of your
waist and the flare of your hips, the smooth line of
your shoulders and the soft gleam of your skin in the
light.''

Words failed her.

Heart pounding, she could only stare up at this man
who could be questioning one minute and gentle the
next. For a second she wished she could be part of his
family and their obvious love for one another.

Or maybe she wanted more. She could imagine his
caring for someone. The safety of his arms and the
sweetness of his caresses would be something to write
home about. She could tell Adam she was totally
safe....

''What are you thinking?'' he demanded, leaning
closer to gaze into her eyes.

She shook her head, unable to answer. Longing engulfed her, a mixture of need for his comforting touch,
desire for his passion and hunger for his nurturing
ways. His love for a woman would be deep and protective and forever.

For a moment she wanted that. For a space between
one thought and the next, she lived in the fantasy that
he could be hers. All she had to do was reach out.

He caught her hand before she could touch his
chest. ''You're either the best actress in the world, or
you're the most vulnerable person I ever met.''

She pulled back from the brink of madness. ''Which
do you think I am?''

He heaved an exasperated breath. "Damned if I know."

She saw the worry in his eyes and knew it was for his family. The waitress outfit and ridiculous makeup, plus the way she'd skipped out of Vegas, would make anyone suspicious of her motives. She regretted she couldn't tell him the whole truth. After all, he was a lawman and should be safe.

No! Adam had stressed the importance of not trusting anyone for any reason. She had to keep her worries to herself. That was the first rule of survival.

"My uncle thinks you're worried about something," her host continued as if reading her thoughts.

The pause when he finished speaking was calculated to invite her confidence. "I'm not. Well, only the usual things," she amended with a bland smile.

It came to her that lying to this man could be a danger in itself. If caught, there would be the devil to pay.

He stared at her another second as if puzzled about something, then nodded and left the room, closing the door silently behind him. Honey sank onto the bed, feeling as if she'd walked over hot coals without being burned.

"The devil to pay?" she murmured. She was pretty sure she knew who that devil was.

Honey eyed Sal, the mare she was to ride. "I hope you know what you're doing," she said to the blaze-faced cow pony. "I certainly don't."

It was morning and they were going on the tour Zack had promised the previous night. From the open stable door, one of the twins watched them with a smile. He waved when he caught her eye.

She nodded, then concentrated on getting into the saddle without making a fool of herself. She took a deep breath, then made a leap of faith, hoping she'd land on the horse the way Zack had demonstrated to her a moment ago.

"Good," he said when, to her amazement, she found she was on top of the horse, facing forward, her legs on either side as they were supposed to be.

She grinned, as much in surprise as pleasure at her accomplishment. "Lay on, Macduff," she quoted from some Shakespearean play she recalled from high school, settling both feet firmly in the stirrups.

Her escort gave her a quizzical, oblique glance that stole her breath away. In snug jeans and boots, a blue T-shirt showing at the neck of a plaid cotton shirt, he looked like a movie star on location, playing the town marshal who took on a whole gang of baddies.

The gun at his side wasn't a prop, though. It was the type law-enforcement officers carried and reminded her that his job was dangerous, although probably not as dangerous as her brother's.

She saw his eyes on her face, then her hair and the hat he'd given her to wear. His uncle had peered at her hair at the breakfast table that morning in the same manner, as if puzzled by something.

Should she touch up the roots?

She'd added brown-black along her temples and the uneven part after she'd bleached the strands platinum-blond. She thought it made an effective disguise. Surely no one would suspect a natural ash-blonde of dyeing her hair and darkening the roots.

Zack led the way to the stock fence at the end of the road. He opened and closed the gate without dismounting. She was impressed and said so.

"The mare knows how to do that," he told her. "All you have to do is nudge her in the right side with your heel when you get close to a gate. She'll do the rest."

Honey laughed. "She might not understand my signals."

He gave her a few more tips on riding and concluded, "Grab the saddle horn if you get into trouble."

Again he gave her a sideways, assessing glance before leading them across the pasture. Hundreds of bovine eyes observed their progress.

"How many cows do you have?" she asked as a group broke and ran to the far side of the field when they approached.

"Ranchers call them cattle or beeves. Cows are females. Males are steers or bulls."

"Okay. How many *cattle* do you have?"

"We run a breeding herd of five hundred cows. Steers, another five hundred or so, are raised as heavy Western beeves for the restaurant market."

She absorbed this information. "Why are they called 'heavy Western'?"

"That's what they are. Most calves are sold when they're around six months old. Some steers are kept longer in order to develop more, so they're bigger when they go to market. They're great for steaks and prime ribs."

Looking at the calves frolicking in the sun near their mothers, she wasn't sure she'd ever eat another steak.

"Don't humanize them," he advised, following her train of thought. "They're animals."

"So are we."

"Yeah, but we carry the guns."

That brought her worries plunging down on her shoulders like a bucket of hot coals. Gazing at the splendid isolation of the mountains, she realized she did feel safer here. Nothing terrible could happen amidst such beauty.

Zack pulled up on a rise that gave a clear view of the land. "Look," he said, sweeping his hand in an inviting gesture, as if he presented a gift beyond price.

The scene was so inviting she experienced a return of the yearning that occasionally caused an ache in her chest. She didn't understand what she wanted so desperately that it made her hurt. Her earliest memories included this odd longing for things she couldn't name.

Once as a teenager, when she tried to tell Adam about the ache, he'd given her the saddest smile. She'd known then that he felt it, too.

It must be something to do with being orphans, she'd decided at that time, and missing their parents.

Looking at the homestead below, she knew that was part of it, but not all. Zack's uncle had taken in several orphans and made a home for them. In spite of his own loss, his heart had been big enough to include others. The three brothers obviously loved their uncle and the ranch they called home. She was sure the other cousins did, too.

A family was what one made of it, she concluded. It could be happiness and security, or it could be resentment and little acts of meanness such as she'd known from her own cousin. She envied Zack his relatives.

He touched the underside of her chin and turned her face toward him. "What makes you so sad?"

She sensed the probing intelligence behind the question even though he spoke in a quiet way.

"I'm not," she immediately denied, lifting her chin and leaning away from him. The mare stirred restlessly and pranced sideways.

"A horse reacts to emotion," he warned, his eyes dissecting her every thought. "They always know when their rider is troubled."

She stared at the scenery and said nothing.

"What bothers you about being here?"

Her hands jerked on the reins at the softly worded question. The mare backed up a step, giving a nervous whinny as she did and tossing her head.

Zack patted the animal on the neck. "Easy, girl," he murmured, but his eyes were on Honey.

She stared at his hand as he stroked the brown hide. If she was to confide in him, then what?

She had no doubt that he knew how to wield the gun he carried, but surely no one could find her here. If the time came when she felt she'd put his family in danger, she would tell him. Truly she would. That was only fair.

But now wasn't that time, and she was reluctant to admit her deception.

She turned an innocent smile on him. ''Why should anything be bothering me? The morning is too perfect for mundane worries. Can we ride to that ridge up there?''

He looked at where she pointed. ''Yes. It's an easy trail. Loosen up on the reins a bit. The mare will follow my horse with no problem.''

True to his word, she found the winding trail an easy upward climb. The mare stayed on the path with no real direction from her. At the moment, she was hurting no one, so she relegated any problems to the darkest corners of her mind and let herself enjoy the beauty.

''We'll give the horses a rest here,'' Zack said an hour later, coming into a secluded clearing lush with a carpet of late-summer growth.

After they dismounted, he looped the reins over some shrubs and loosened the saddles. She followed him up the trail until they came out on a level slab of granite. A flat-topped boulder, about eight feet high and ten feet in diameter, sat in the middle of the escarpment.

"The Devil's Dining Room," he announced, and led the way to a round rock about three feet high. "This is his seat. Here, put your foot in my hands and I'll lift you up."

She did as ordered. In a second she was on the boulder and could see for miles in all directions. Zack stepped on the smaller rock and hoisted himself up beside her. When he sat on the side and dangled his legs over the edge, she did the same.

"It's warm up here," she marveled, removing her coat and folding it into a square to use as a cushion.

"The wind isn't blowing. It gets pretty brisk across this ridge at times, then you get the chill."

"Is this part of the Seven Devils mountain range?"

"Yes. It mostly runs north and south. To the west is the Hells Canyon of the Snake River, the deepest gorge in North America."

"I thought the Grand Canyon was."

He shook his head. "The south rim of the Grand Canyon is around 4000 feet, the north rim about 6000. The west rim of Hells Canyon is more than 5600 feet above the river while the other side rises to He-Devil Peak on the east."

"That's over 9000 feet. I remember it from the map. Why are the mountains called Seven Devils?"

"Indian legend. There are seven peaks that stand in a semicircle on the Idaho side of the Snake, all towering 8000 feet or more above the river. The Nez Percé say there were once seven child-eating giant devils living in the Blue Mountains of Oregon. Each year they moved eastward to find more prey. The chiefs asked Coyote to help protect their little ones.''

''Did he?'' she asked when Zack paused.

''Yes. Coyote and Fox devised a plan whereby all the animals with claws dug seven very deep holes and filled them with boiling liquid. When the monsters started their next journey eastward, they fell in the holes and couldn't get out. Then Coyote changed them into seven giant mountains as punishment for their wickedness and as a warning to others. He made Hells Canyon so more of their kind couldn't follow.''

Honey couldn't take her eyes from Zack as he recounted the legend, then with his face close to hers, pointed out the peaks rising north of them as far as she could see. To the west and east, the land fell away in layer after layer of geologic faults. She could imagine monsters thrashing about and causing the land to heave and break.

The clean, warm scent of his skin pleased her as she inhaled deeply. He'd shaved that morning, a contrast to yesterday when they'd awoken in the SUV and he'd had a full day's growth of beard on his face.

Slowly he swiveled his head until their faces were only inches apart. He stared into her eyes. An eternity seemed to pass as they looked at each other.

She knew each breath he took. She was aware of her own heartbeat. Silence surrounded them.

He moved closer. Or perhaps she did.

It didn't matter.

When their lips met, she felt herself fall into an abyss of boiling liquid. It didn't burn, although she was filled with unbearable heat. Needs that she'd ignored for years poured forth.

She heard a low moan and realized it came from her.

At once his arms swept around her, bringing them closer. Their bodies moved as one, pivoting toward each other so that flesh met flesh, fire met fire, hunger met hunger. It was wonderful…and frightening.

"Please," she whispered, knowing she shouldn't be feeling this, shouldn't be wanting this man.

"What?" he asked. "What do you want?"

He stroked her cheek with one hand and held the back of her head with the other, his caress gentle but arousing, his lips against her cheek.

She sighed shakily and turned her head, severing the contact. Her lips burned, but she wanted more. She forced herself to stillness.

Slowly he let her go.

"That was enlightening," he murmured, something of wonder and a bit of amusement in his voice.

She searched for a defense against him and the passion. "I might be your cousin," she reminded him, a barrier against the mutual desire.

The blue eyes, mysteriously dark, deeply questioning, narrowed as he searched her face. "Are you?"

She tried to lie but couldn't. She shrugged.

He wrapped a loose curl around his finger. She realized her hat had fallen behind her somewhere. His, too, had disappeared. "What if I've changed my mind about that?" he asked.

She thought of her promise to her brother and the need to stay out of sight. If she wasn't Zack's cousin, she would have to leave. "Y-you can't," she stuttered.

His gaze went darker, moodier. "Why not?"

Her mind scurried for a reason. "The passion. It's too…" She searched for a word.

"Dangerous?"

"It could be." Looking down at her clasped hands, she fought a mad, compelling urge to simply give herself over to him and let fate decide the next course.

He let out an audible breath. "So you admit you feel it, too?"

"Yes, but passion can be a two-edged sword," she warned. "And it has no place between us."

"You're right. It can cut both ways and hurt others, too," he murmured. "It has no place between us if we're truly cousins." He handed her the hat and put his on.

It took a second for his doubtful tone to register with her. "You *have* changed your mind."

"Let's just say I'm less certain than I was when we were in Vegas. It's a city of mirages. The mountain air has a way of clearing a person's head of illusions."

She scrambled to her feet as panic set in. "Does this mean you want me to leave?" she asked coolly, riding a wave of righteous anger to hide her sudden fear that he would tell her to go.

He rose, standing six inches taller than her five feet, eight inches. For a long, grueling moment, he studied her without answering, then he said, "No. You've kept your part of the bargain. Uncle Nick would like you to stay."

When he leaped off the rock, then turned and held up his arms for her, she stood there as if turned to stone.

Glancing at the distant peaks, she thought of the monsters who'd been punished for their sins. What would fate decide was just punishment for her lies and evasions?

"Come," he said.

She sat on the ledge and pushed herself off the boulder. He caught her easily, his strength sure and dependable, and set her on her feet.

"I came because I wanted to get away," she said, unable to keep from telling him this much of the truth.

"From what?" he demanded softly, his hands on her shoulders.

"The frying pan," she said with a rueful grimace. "Vegas was too hot."

His smile mocked the heated attraction between them. "Ah, but you forget—fire is a potent weapon... to a devil."

A shiver rushed down her spine.

Chapter Five

Honey ignored the feeling of abandonment when Zack left for work shortly after lunch. He hadn't said whether he'd come back to the ranch or stay in town for the night.

She looked at photo albums with his uncle. There were pictures of the young Tink and her parents, the orphaned cousins and their parents. Honey found it all very moving.

The temperature climbed to eighty-three that afternoon. The sun was bright and the landscape inviting. When Uncle Nick went to his room for a nap, she donned a pair of boots to go with her jeans and shirt, then slipped outside for a stroll about the immediate area.

The mare rushed to the fence as soon as Honey came within sight. She scratched the animal's ears, then, tracking an unhappy sound, she found six calves in a pen beside the barn. They rushed to the gate and bawled excitedly when she leaned over the fence to admire them.

Carefully she opened the gate and went inside, making sure the latch was secure behind her. She didn't want to cause trouble and give Zack an excuse to scold her, but the calves were so cute, she just had to pet them.

When she reached down to scratch the nearest set of ears, the calf grabbed her finger and sucked strongly. Another latched on to her sleeve while a third pulled on the fabric of her shirttail. The other three gathered around and nuzzled her hips and legs in search of—she assumed—a serving of cow's milk.

Laughing, she rubbed their heads and tried to tell one from the other while they jostled for position. All six were red-brown with white blazes down their faces and white stockings.

When they nearly knocked her off her feet, she pushed her way to the fence and, shooing them off, scooted out the gate and closed it before any could escape. Her shirt and pants had wet patches all along the bottom edges.

"I see you got acquainted with the calves," one of the twins said.

"A bit more than I expected. They seemed to think

I was a milk cow.'' She studied him, seeking a clue to his identity, then gave up. ''Which twin are you?''

''Travis, the quiet, ugly one.''

His smile was kind. She liked the quiet depths of him and wondered if that came naturally or as part of the hurt when his wife and child died.

''Are there any identifying marks I should look for so I'll know who's who?'' she asked.

''Not where a person could check in public,'' Trevor informed her, coming out of the barn and giving her a wink. ''I got a fish hook caught in my rear once and still have the scar to prove it.''

''From your pole or someone else's?''

''Mine,'' he confessed. ''I tried to blame Trav, but the line led directly to the end of my rod. I thought I had a fish at first, then I noticed every time I yanked, I got this terrible pain in the behind.''

''Yeah, but it took him three tries before he figured out he'd caught himself,'' Travis added.

She laughed at the story, then gestured toward the calves. ''Why are these little ones here, instead of in the pasture with their mamas?''

''These were orphaned at birth or the mother rejected them,'' Travis explained. ''We bring 'em up here and raise them by hand. When you went into the pen, they thought you were going to feed them.''

At once her heart went out to the calves, who crowded against the gate and mooed hopeful calls for attention from the humans.

''How do you feed them?''

"With a special bucket," Travis told her. "We also have several orphaned lambs and twin colts to feed. You want to watch tonight when we do the chores?"

"Yes, if you don't mind. I've never been on a ranch. It all seems so fascinating."

Trevor, the more outgoing one of the twins, chuckled, his expression rueful. "Especially at ten below zero with a west wind cutting through your clothes, and you're out looking for some dumb critters that found a hole in the fence and decided to go exploring. Yep, fascinating is how I've always described it, haven't you, brother?"

Travis solemnly agreed he had.

Honey had to laugh. "City slickers always have an idealized view of the ranching life," she admitted.

"We're going out to ride fences and look for breaks," Trevor continued. "You want to tag along?"

She shook her head. "That's kind of you, but I'm already feeling the effects of the ride Zack and I went on this morning."

That brought identical grins from the twins. "Just wait until tomorrow morning," Trevor warned. "You'll discover muscles you didn't know you had. Get out of bed carefully."

"I will. Thanks for the warning."

On that cheerful note, the twins returned to the barn. In a few minutes she watched them leave in a pickup, rolls of barbed wire stacked in the back along with fence posts and a large tool box. A horse trailer with two saddled mounts was attached to the truck.

She waved when they did and stayed by the fence with the calves. After the truck was out of sight, she roamed the rest of the homestead area.

Again following sounds, she discovered the orphaned lambs housed in an adjoining stable. She reached over the slats and petted them rather than going inside one of the stalls, having learned that lesson with the calves. She found they wanted to suckle, too.

"Poor little spoiled babies," she murmured, loving the feel of their warm, fluffy bodies.

Slowly she made her way around the place until she knew every building and every pasture and the animals they contained. To her surprise, she found chickens in a fenced area. Stepping carefully over the bare dirt, she peered inside the building there and found it filled with roosting boxes filled with straw. Several hens studied her balefully.

Honey washed off her boots at an outside spigot to dislodge any signs of her sojourn around the animals, then removed them at the door to the house and left them on the porch. Inside she found Uncle Nick working on ledgers and watching a cable news show on TV.

"How about a cup of hot tea?" he asked, surprising her.

"That would be nice, but I'll get it for us."

"You'll find cups and tea bags in the kitchen. I heat the water in the microwave."

In the cupboard she found several different types of herbal teas. She chose one with hibiscus leaves and green tea, then prepared two cups. "Do you take sugar?" she called from the kitchen.

"Nope, just straight."

She brought the cups into the living room and set one on the old-fashioned rolltop desk. A laptop computer was nestled inside, along with a printer and fax machine.

"All the modern conveniences," she said. "It doesn't go with my vision of a ranch."

His eyes twinkled. "We used to be the film version of a homestead. The county didn't run electric lines out this way until the 1950s. We had to pay for the wire and poles to reach the main road from the house."

"That must have been expensive."

"Most ranchers felled their own trees for the poles and set them. We went in together to buy the wire in bulk and then strung most of it ourselves."

"How long has your family owned the ranch?"

"Since shortly after the Civil War. My ancestors came West to start a new life."

"Zack said they were from the good Daltons, not the outlaw gang."

"Yeah, but one of them nearly got hanged just for being a Dalton. Back in those days, posses didn't always ask a lot of questions before stringing a man up."

For the rest of the afternoon and into the evening, Uncle Nick told her stories of his ancestors and others who came West to make their fortunes. She peeled potatoes while he put a chicken in the oven to bake. She commented on his skill in the house.

"A man needs to know how to get along on his own," he told her. "All the boys know how to cook," he added with a sly smile in her direction.

Honey got a little flustered as she thought of Zack and his serving her a steaming cup of coffee in the makeshift bed in the back of the SUV. He would make some lucky girl a good husband.

But not her. Her life was like a tumbleweed's, moving from one place to another.

The twins returned and reported their progress to their uncle. When Honey went outside to watch the feeding of the orphans, she envisioned the fresh new life the pioneers had sought as they left all they knew and headed for this rough, unsettled country. She would have liked to be one of them. To find a home here would be worth any hardship.

"Here, feed one of the calves," Travis invited.

He handed her a bucket with a big nipple attached to the side near the bottom.

At her look, he laughed. "Did you think we held them in our arms on their backs and used baby bottles?"

"Well, sort of. I didn't realize they ate this much." She lugged the bucket into the pen and nearly got tumbled from her feet by the eager orphans.

Travis gave the more obnoxious ones a slap on the rear to get them out of the way and hung two buckets on hooks where the little ones could reach them. He went back inside to prepare more buckets for the other three babies.

Honey's calf sucked lustily on the rubber nipple and gazed at her with adoring eyes the whole time. She stroked its head and touched the spot where the hair formed a whorl in the middle of its forehead.

Something painful tugged at her insides.

She knew she was being sentimental about the animals, but babies of all species were so sweetly appealing. She wondered how it would be to hold her own baby and maybe sing a lullaby while it nursed.

Inhaling deeply as the odd sensations inside her increased, she acknowledged that babies weren't something she thought a lot about. There'd never been enough time in her life to consider making a family of her own.

She and Adam had worked after school and on weekends. It was he who'd noted her love of dancing and arranged for lessons and paid for them, too, until she was old enough to earn her own money and pay her own way. Her aunt had been furious at the ''waste of time and money,'' but Adam had prevailed in their arguments about the lessons.

All that she was she owed to him.

Later that night she hooked her laptop into the telephone line in her bedroom and checked her e-mails. There was none from Adam. She sent him a coded advertisement that told him she'd arrived at the ranch safely.

When she heard a vehicle shortly before eleven, she

peered out the window and spotted Zack's arrival. She watched him get out of the police cruiser, stretch as if weary, then glance at her window. He stopped at the edge of the sidewalk and stared in her direction.

She realized he had seen her.

Her heart set up a terrible racket, beating harder and faster than she'd ever experienced. She dropped the curtain and stepped away from the window, but she knew he could still detect her form with the light behind her on the night table and only the lace and glass between them.

When he knocked softly on her door, she debated whether she should open it. It was late, and her emotions were raw and vulnerable for reasons that had to do with the babies she'd fed that evening and the loneliness she'd felt upon thinking about her brother.

Not to mention the attraction that jolted her each time she thought of Zack, who had given her a safe harbor just when she needed it. The late hour, the isolation and the desire could lead to a most dangerous situation.

Moreover, she mustn't confuse gratitude with deeper feelings.

The knock came again, a sharp rat-a-tat-tat that demanded entrance. She breathed deeply, checked that her robe was tied securely over her nightgown and opened the door.

''Yes?'' she said.

Zack couldn't take his eyes off Honey. Her hair fell in waves to her shoulders. She looked very feminine in a pink satin nightgown and robe with little rosebuds embroidered on the material in a random fashion. Her face was bare of makeup and her mouth was a soft, natural pink.

His heart set up a raucous beat, so loud he was afraid she would hear it and get the wrong idea. Or maybe get the right idea.

Cool it. He was not bowled over by this mysterious female with her intriguing, contradictory ways. So there was an air of vulnerability about her. She needed his protection like a python needed legs. A wise man kept his emotions in check.

"What is it?" she asked, her eyes dark in the dim light, then flashing silver as she moved back to let him in.

He stepped inside and closed the door, then leaned against it. "I saw your light and realized you were still up. I like a cup of something hot when I get home, especially when the air has a nip to it."

While it was hot during the day, nights at this altitude usually dropped into the forties. It was forty-two tonight although it had been in the eighties during the day.

"If this is a nip, I'd hate to see a bite," she joked, wrapping her arms across her chest and giving a mock shiver.

He laughed, pleased by the unexpected humor for reasons he couldn't pin down. "Tea or hot chocolate?"

"Umm, Uncle Nick and I had tea this afternoon. Perhaps cocoa would be nice."

"You got it."

Zack led the way to the main part of the house. After hanging up his hat and pulling off his boots, he prepared the hot cocoa, aware of Honey's eyes on him in a questioning way the whole time.

"What did you do while I was gone?" he asked.

"Looked at photos of your family, listened to stories about the past while peeling potatoes and learned to feed the orphans when the twins returned from mending fences. I also learned there's a lot of work associated with a ranch."

"Yeah, it isn't all singing songs around a camp-fire."

She laughed softly, eliciting a funny pang from deep within his gut. Travis had once told him that the lone-liest moment of his life was returning to the house and knowing his wife was no longer there, that she would never again be there, waiting to welcome him home.

Zack, for the first time, had an inkling of what his brother meant. This late-night sharing of cocoa and the day's adventures was intimate in ways he'd never experienced with a woman, not even those whose bed he'd shared.

"So how was your day?" she asked.

"Okay, I guess. We had a couple of bank robberies, a shoot-out at the corral and a brawl at the saloon when the ladies' temperance league tried to close the place down."

"I must have missed something when we drove through town, such as the bank, the saloon *and* the corral."

When he shifted and his foot touched hers, hot tongues of need flashed up his leg and into his groin. Like him, she was in her socks.

"Were you doing some work on the computer?" he asked.

She looked startled. "What?"

"There was a laptop in your room. I thought maybe you were sending some e-mails or balancing your checkbook."

He watched her closely. The vibes she was sending were those of sudden wariness. They matched the expression of caution that flitted over her face.

"Oh, that." She shrugged. "I thought I'd better let my aunt and cousin know I'd arrived safely."

She was lying.

He knew it. Anger added to the tumult of hunger coursing through his blood. He hated being lied to. "Or were you letting some friend or friends know the layout of the place?" he suggested, watching her every move.

Her confusion looked genuine. "I'm not following you."

"If someone was in trouble, the ranch would make a good hideaway. It's isolated, difficult to get to…and the locals take people at their word."

Understanding dawned in her eyes. For a second he

detected pain coupled with panic, then decided it was a mirage as she spoke in a tight and angry tone.

"You're right," she said. "I sent an e-mail to every crook in Vegas, telling them I'd found the perfect getaway."

For a long minute she held his gaze without blinking, then she picked up her half-full cup, poured the contents down the drain, put the cup in the dishwasher and left the room without looking back.

He felt like a heel.

Damn, how was it a woman could make a man feel guilty without uttering a word? Still, she'd given him reason to be suspicious with her camouflage as a boy when they left Vegas and her evasive manner of answering questions, as if she mulled over how much truth to inject into her replies.

Anyway, he'd been surprised by the laptop computer he'd spotted in her room. He didn't know why. Lots of people kept in touch by e-mail these days. It was just that she'd seemed so *alone* in the world.

Or was that what she wanted him to think?

He sighed and wished he'd spent the night in town.

Honey awoke at six. The sun was already up. It seemed to rise earlier on the ranch than in the city. Of course in the city she worked at night, so she was rarely awake to greet the sunrise.

Her spirits were heavy as she swung her legs out of bed, then gave an involuntary groan. The muscles of her thighs and rear protested each movement. She managed to wash up, dress and hobble down to the kitchen.

Zack and his uncle were at the table, each with a cup of coffee. They were talking earnestly and quietly, so she couldn't make out the words. They stopped when they spotted her in the living room.

"Ah, you're up," Uncle Nick said. "Come join us. There're flapjacks in the oven. I made the boys leave some for you, but it was a fight."

She smiled at the older man and managed not to look at Zack as she greeted them. She retrieved her breakfast from the warm oven, poured milk and coffee and sat at the table between the two men.

"Zack and I were just talking about keeping you busy while you're here. Since you seem taken with the animals, I thought you could take over the care of the orphans," Uncle Nick told her. "That would save the twins some time."

"I'd love to," she said sincerely.

"They have to be fed twice a day," Zack warned her. "Every morning and night."

She took umbrage at the obvious doubt in his tone. Hoisting her chin a notch, she told him, "I can do it."

"Show her how to check for worms. And pink eye," the older man ordered. He stood. "I got laundry to do."

After he left the room, the silence was intense.

"Look, I'm sorry about last night," Zack said. "I didn't mean to imply—"

"Yes, you did." She swallowed a bite of pancake

without tasting it. "You suspect me of skullduggery. I'm not sure why. You're the one who insisted I come up here."

He gave her a frustrated once-over as if trying to figure her out. She held his gaze without flinching.

His smile was disarming. "Being around you gets me mixed-up. Let's call a truce, okay? Do you really want to learn about the care and feeding of the animals?"

She nodded.

"Fine. The twins have already fed them this morning. You can do it tonight. In the meantime, I thought we'd help them check the herd for a couple of hours."

"On horseback?"

"Yes."

She held up both hands in protest. "No way."

He had the nerve to laugh. "I thought I heard a groan when you sat down. Travis advised me to take it easy on you today. Sore, huh?"

She leveled a look at him without answering.

Giving her a wise glance, he added, "Riding is the only way to work it out."

"Huh," she said skeptically.

His eyes met hers. He smiled. So did she. Then they laughed at the same time. And just like that, the tension between them dissolved.

"It's going to be warm today. I have a jacket you can use while you're here. You looked like an outlaw running around in that trench coat. In the Wild West days, gunmen wore those to conceal their weapons."

"Since I don't have any weapons, it would hardly apply."

"Oh, yes, you do," he said, giving her a sexy once-over. "Eat up and we'll go."

Ignoring the heat that raced through her veins, she finished the meal and set out on her new adventure at Zack's heels. He assigned two horses for her use.

She learned to saddle her own mount and to mix the various powders with water for the calves, lambs and the two colts whose mother had gone insane after birth and tried to trample her own offspring. She'd never heard of anything like that and said so.

"All mammals share a lot of the same characteristics," he told her. "We carry the seeds of our own destruction within us."

She wondered if he was thinking of his parents, or perhaps of someone he'd loved and lost.

"Hey, are you two going to help?" Trevor called. "We're counting calves. Cut out part of the herd, do the count and then move them into the far west pasture."

"Yeah, we'll help. Stay close," Zack told her. "I'll cut and you count."

Once they began, she forgot the kinks in her muscles. Within an hour, she'd removed the jacket and tied it around her waist. She pulled the borrowed cowboy hat low on her forehead the way Zack did so the wind wouldn't catch the brim and blow it off, then concentrated on her job.

Zack cut out about twenty cows at a time. She

counted the calves, then rode at the back of the little group while he opened a gate and drove them through. By the time they went in for lunch, the task was finished.

"You shoulda seen our new hand here," Trevor told Uncle Nick as they sat down to heaping bowls of rice, stir-fry vegetables and tenderloin. "She was working like a pro by the end of the first hour."

"After she got through groaning with every step," Zack interjected with an oblique glance her way.

Honey basked in their teasing. It was good-natured and inclusive, as if she was a welcome addition to the family. As if her contribution to the work had been necessary. As if she belonged to this warm clan of Daltons.

"I knew she would take to riding and herding," Uncle Nick said with great certainty. "Tink could ride like a pro when she was only three."

A beat of silence passed, then, "I understand you're a dancer," Trevor said kindly, changing the subject.

"Yes, well, I was." She was forced to repeat the story about the company folding.

For the rest of the meal she was peppered with questions about the dance troupe and about dancing as a career. From the Daltons, it didn't feel intrusive. They seemed fascinated with her answers.

"Did you go to a dance school?" Zack asked.

"First I went to a local dance teacher who held classes in a small strip mall. When I was fifteen, she recommended me to the artistic director of a dance company. I auditioned and was accepted.''

"You must have been good to become part of their group when you were still a teenager."

She smiled. "I was accepted for training. The next year I got to dance in the chorus for special performances. I still had to go to school, so my time was limited. And I had chores at home."

Falling silent, she recalled the taunts from her cousin when she practiced her routines in front of the full-length mirror Adam had mounted on her closet door.

"Do you get some kind of degree or certificate for dancing?" Uncle Nick asked.

"Not with a dance company, but you do gain credentials. My teacher studied under a teacher who studied under Martha Graham. Being a member of a well-known company can be enough recognition to open doors for a dancer, or being good enough to study under a Graham or Balanchine."

"It's like a lineage," Zack said in a musing tone, "the way top Thoroughbreds can be traced back to three Arabian stallions."

Honey experienced a flush of pleasure as the men nodded in unison and looked approvingly at her as if she had prime bloodlines. She didn't even mind the comparison of her dancing credentials with horse breeding.

Chapter Six

After Zack left for work and the twins went back to their chores, Honey and Uncle Nick walked around the homestead while he checked on the progress of the work on the ranch and explained its operations to her.

"Ah, here come the chickens," he said at one point.

She followed his line of sight and spotted a delivery truck with a plume of dust rising behind it.

"Young fool. He's driving too fast, but they all do," Uncle Nick said in disgust.

They crossed the road to the house in time to meet the vehicle. The driver hopped out with the engine running. "Hey, Mr. Dalton, got your chicks." He placed two cartons on the sidewalk. Indignant peeps issued from the boxes.

"I thought as much." Uncle Nick nodded toward the lane. "You were going pretty fast for a country road. You want to be on guard for washouts. We've had some storms, you know."

"Yes, sir, Mr. Dalton. I'll remember," the young man, who looked to be in his early twenties, promised. He smiled at Honey as he handed the older man the delivery receipt to sign. "Who's this?"

"A guest. Zack brought her. Honey Carrington. Danny Ribona." Uncle Nick wrote his name and handed the clipboard back to the rather brash delivery-man.

Honey saw the immediate speculation in Danny's eyes and wondered at Uncle Nick's words. He made it sound as if she belonged to Zack. At this idea, a shiver danced along her back, which irritated her. Zack Dalton was nothing to her, nor she to him.

"Is Zack bringing you to the dance Saturday night?" the young man wanted to know.

"Probably," the uncle answered before she could.

Danny grinned. "Save me one." With a wave, he jumped into the truck and headed back down the road, the plume of dust trailing behind him.

Honey carried the cartons to the hen enclosure under the older man's directions.

"Danny was kind of a wild one in school," he told her, "but he seems to have straightened out since he left home and got a steady job. His mother is enough to drive a man crazy. That woman could nag a saint to death."

"Some men need to be nagged. Without women to keep them on the path to civilization, men would still be living in caves," she asserted, tongue-in-cheek.

The uncle chuckled at her declaration. He opened the cartons while she closed the gate.

"Oh!" Honey exclaimed softly. The boxes were filled with tiny baby chicks, each a bundle of yellow fluff.

"There's a place inside for them," he said, leading the way into the henhouse. "I knew you were going to be good for my nephew as soon as I laid eyes on you," he told her.

It took her a few seconds to gather her scattered thoughts. "That's not true. I mean, Zack and I…I'm here because of your daughter and what happened to her. Zack thinks I could be his cousin."

Uncle Nick gave her a shrewd glance. "Do you?" he asked softly, his manner kind but sad, too.

Honey couldn't bring herself to imply she might be. Neither could she tell the truth, although she was seized with a desire to confess all.

Adam had impressed upon her the importance of silence when he became an undercover detective. "Tell no one. Trust no one," he'd ordered. "Every law-enforcement agency has some bad eggs in it. A chance remark, spoken at the wrong time, can have serious consequences in ways we can't imagine at that moment."

Without talking to him first, she didn't feel free to discuss her life or her reasons for being in this remote haven with anyone. If word somehow got back to the bad guys who were searching for Adam, via her, and led to her brother being harmed, she would never forgive herself.

Her brother had been her champion all her life. She could do no less for him. She remained silent.

"Never mind," the older man said gently. "I'm glad you came to us."

They made the little ones comfortable with food and water in a corner of the building fenced off with chicken wire from the rest, then returned to the ranch house.

After Uncle Nick went to his room for a nap, she sat on the front porch, her back to the sun, and basked in its warmth. A cat crossed the road from the stable and sat beside her, its purr comforting.

"He knows," she whispered to the tabby. "Uncle Nick knows I'm not Tink."

Zack was becoming increasingly suspicious of her as more of her life story unfolded under his family's questioning. What was the point of her being there if everyone knew she wasn't the lost cousin?

Of course she could just disappear, and no one would be the wiser about where she went.

A hot pang shot through her, and she acknowledged there were other dangers in her staying with the Daltons. When the time came, she might not want to leave.

The world dimmed ominously.

When she glanced at the sky, she saw clouds had

collected over the mountain peaks and obscured the sun. The air became colder as the clouds thickened. The cat rose, stretched and returned to the stable. Honey went inside and found a book to read.

Later she fed the orphans, who now started mooing, neighing, baaing or clucking as soon as she appeared. It gave her a contented feeling to know they associated her with good things in their lives.

It was nice to be needed, to have another living creature be glad to see you. Small pleasures. She smiled at the thought even as it saddened her, then finished her chores and helped with supper.

When Zack came home, she was still up, reading her book. The others had gone to bed as soon as the weather report was finished. Although the clouds persisted, no rain was forecast for the week.

"Hi," he said, putting his outdoor clothing and boots away as usual.

"Hi." She stood and cinched the belt on her robe more tightly. "We had apple cobbler for dessert. Uncle Nick said it was your favorite. Would you like some?"

He flashed her a thousand-watt smile. "Sure. Are there any leftovers? I didn't get a chance to eat tonight. There was a wreck on the highway."

He followed her into the kitchen and took a seat at the table while she prepared a plate. "Was anyone hurt?" she asked.

"Some tourists and a local guy, Danny Ribona."

Her eyes went wide. "I met him today. He delivered

some baby chickens to your uncle. Your uncle got after him for driving too fast.''

"That's the guy. However, the accident wasn't his fault. Another car turned left in front of him. Perhaps if he'd been going a tad slower, he could have avoided it. But I doubt it. The accident happened too fast.''

"Is he going to be okay?''

"He has a broken arm, but otherwise is fine. Two other cars were involved. A couple of people had some bruises and scrapes, but nothing life-threatening. Their cars are pretty bad, though. It took a couple of hours to get them towed and the road clear.''

As she set a plate in front of him after heating the food in the microwave, she realized how intimate the scene was. Like last night, they shared the events of the day.

She stood. "I'd better go to bed…to my room,'' she corrected, wishing she hadn't mentioned the bed. It conjured up images better left alone.

"Stay,'' he murmured. "Just while I eat.''

Wondering what had happened to her common sense, she resumed her seat. He finished the meal, then a huge bowl of cobbler with ice cream. Conversation was an effort now as tension filled the room.

She was aware of the hour, the quiet of the house and the warmth within it compared to the outdoors. As soon as he scooped out the last bite, she leaped to her feet and put the dishes in the dishwasher and wiped down all the counters and the table.

"Enough,'' he said when she looked around for

something else to do. His hand clamped around her wrist.

Fire shot up her arm. She stared up at him, hunger and worry that he could make her feel this way running riot through her.

"I want you." He frowned as if he, too, rejected the idea of involvement between them.

"It's ridiculous," she told him sternly, trying to find a defense against the passion. "We can't let this happen."

"I know."

He looked savage, a man driven to the edge and willing to meet trouble head-on, if necessary. With a little shake of his head, he tightened his hold on her wrist. Slowly he drew her closer until there was only an inch between them.

She felt his heat through the thin material of her gown and robe. Golden arcs of awareness flashed between them.

"I'm afraid of this," she told him honestly. "Of needing someone."

"You think I'm not?" he demanded softly.

"For men, it's physical—"

"Not always," he interrupted in a low growl. "Sometimes we have feelings, too."

She swallowed hard as she considered what those feelings might be. "An involvement is impossible."

"And probably irresponsible. And unwise. I agree." He paused, then added, "But when I'm near you, I forget all that. It would be good between us."

Staring into his hard, candid gaze, she nodded. ''While it lasted.''

''We have the rest of the month. Unless you're thinking of leaving earlier?''

''I should.''

Because they both knew she wasn't his cousin, although neither was quite willing to admit it yet, some totally honest part of herself informed her consciousness.

''Yeah,'' he agreed, but obviously with only a small part of his attention. The rest was focused on her mouth, and leaving was far from her mind or his.

He gave a little tug and she fell into his arms—or maybe dived into them was more accurate.

When she looped her arms around his shoulders, he curved his body to fit hers, bending her back over one arm while he cupped a hand behind her neck to steady her for the kiss that was coming.

When his mouth touched hers, she gave herself over to the embrace, forgetting everything but the fulfillment of sharing this with him.

His hand stroked her neck and shoulder, then moved down her arm. He found the opening of the sleeve and slipped his hand inside, caressing to her elbow and back to her wrist.

His hands were strong, his touch gentle. His hunger was great and urgent. She'd never known passion could be coupled with such tenderness. Her lips moved under his, answering each movement and sweet, subtle pressure. Her heart became light, as if it danced upon moonbeams.

Turning her face, she laid her head against his chest and listened to the thunder of his heart while she regained her breath. "I could weep," she whispered. "It's that strong."

"Yes."

He smoothed her hair, then thrust his fingers into the strands and closed them into a fist. He kissed her temple. "There's a dance in town on Saturday night, a fund-raiser for the Historical Society. I bought two tickets. Would you like to go?"

Tilting her head back, she gave him a worried perusal while her stubborn heart leaped with joy. "I shouldn't, but yes, I would love to go."

His chest moved against hers. He was laughing. "We're a couple of fools," he told her, and kissed her on the nose. "Nothing has to be this serious. We'll go to the dance and have fun. Nothing more."

He stepped back and held up his hands in a gesture meant to indicate innocence. But she knew better. There was nothing innocent in the way they responded to each other.

Passion, longing, needing another person, all could be dangerous. Most dangerous of all were the men who were looking for her in order to trap her brother. If they found her, Zack and his family would also be in danger.

She hadn't completely considered their welfare when she'd agreed to come here. Idaho had seemed so far removed from reality. Worry ate at her, for Zack, for his uncle, for the twins, for all the Dalton family.

"What troubles you?" Zack asked.

She shook her head, unable to answer, surprised by his discernment. She had to guard her thoughts more closely.

"It'll be okay," he said after a moment. "I'll make sure of that. You don't have to worry about this thing between us."

It was a promise. For a second she believed him, even though he had no idea of the real problem, had no idea it wasn't simply him and her and their hunger for each other.

When she moved away, he let her go.

In the pretty rose bedroom, she closed the door and flicked on the computer. She wanted to know how much longer Adam thought this would go on. She suddenly, desperately wanted to be free of intrigue and doubts. She wanted a normal life.

For a Friday night the town was quiet. Zack sat at his desk and did the paperwork he'd been neglecting. Finished, he checked the time and saw he still had an hour before his supper break. Since the sheriff's department worked a four-days-on, four-days-off schedule, he'd have four days of freedom starting tomorrow.

Thinking of the dance tomorrow night and the tension between Honey and him, he wondered if he was a glutton for punishment. Maybe he should avoid her.

Okay, so he didn't like that idea. But he'd been the one to introduce her to his family, and that meant he had to keep an eye on her. Besides, Uncle Nick had ordered him to.

Considering all the evidence from the moment they'd met, he was positive she was in some kind of trouble. At times he detected fear in the depths of her eyes. She often seemed worried and easily startled, maybe even guilt-ridden.

If she was using the isolated ranch for safety reasons, at least she had a conscience about it.

The question was, did she represent a danger to Uncle Nick and the twins? Was she hiding out from someone she'd double-crossed?

He couldn't quite believe that of her, but what did he really know about her, other than she had the most kissable mouth of any woman he'd ever met?

Perhaps she'd inadvertently overheard vital information that was incriminating to some crooks. After all, she had been working in a casino. Her obvious worry worried him.

After a few more minutes of mulling over the situation, he looked up a number in his files, picked up the phone and dialed the Las Vegas Police Department. As a cop, he had contacts. As a cop, it was his duty to investigate suspicious happenings.

The detective he'd worked with on the escaped-convict case answered. Zack identified himself and gave the other lawman a rundown of the information he wanted.

"A lost cousin, a waitress and a dancer?" the detective said, amused. "Interesting combination."

"That's what I thought. She's originally from Los Angeles, but came to Vegas with a dance troupe." Zack described the situation as Honey had told it to him. "I don't know how much is true, if any. The casino cop might know more. His name was Bert Vance."

"Hey, I know him," the detective reported. "He'll tell us what he knows. I'll get back to you ASAP. You got an e-mail address?"

"Yeah." Zack gave out the information. He answered a few more questions, then they said goodbye and hung up.

After his shift, when he was heading back to the ranch, he wondered if he'd done the right thing. Investigating a mysterious female who denied being his cousin, but left the question open to interpretation, seemed appropriate, but things were more complicated than that.

Desire. It always clouded the issues.

He was reminded of that when he arrived at the house. The disappointment was acute when he found no one waiting up for him. He wanted to see Honey.

Her windows were dark, so he refrained from knocking on her door and inviting her to share a cup of cocoa. He wanted more than a hot drink. So did she. At least she was honest about that.

Angry with fate, with her and with himself, he went to the room he used when he was home and hit the sack.

Honey considered one outfit, discarded it, then tried another. Clothes were not usually a big thing with her. Her money had gone for dance lessons, leotards and shoes. She realized she should have checked with Zack, since she had no clue what the locals wore to a dance.

Irritated with the uncertainty, she grabbed an ankle-length black skirt and put it on over a black leotard with long sleeves. With three silver chains and silver dangling earrings, she decided she would do. She opened her largest suitcase, the one containing her dance outfits, toe and tap shoes and practice clothing. She chose a pair of black sling-back heels and slipped them on.

With her black trench coat over her arm and a tiny silver purse, she headed down the hall to the living room.

"Wow," Trevor said, clutching his chest. "A vision has arrived. Be still, my heart."

Uncle Nick turned from the TV news and gave her a thorough once-over.

She held her arms out and did a complete turn. "Is this okay? I forgot to ask what people wear for a dance here."

"You look great," a masculine voice said behind her.

Pivoting, she saw Zack. Her heart turned over as

she gazed into his vivid blue eyes. His hair fell in a dark sweep across his forehead, making her want to run her fingers through the shiny strands.

He wore black slacks and a jacket of dressy black leather over a blue shirt left casually open at the neck. When she inhaled, she caught a whiff of his cologne.

"Ready?" he asked.

She nodded.

"Don't wait up," he advised his relatives.

He laid a hand on the small of her back and ushered her toward the door as the others wished them a good time. Honey tried not to read anything into the evening. She refused to call it a date. They were going to a fund-raiser, so it was a charity event. That was all.

And if she believed that, someone might manage to sell her the Brooklyn Bridge before the night was over.

"Here, put your coat on," Zack told her. "It's cool tonight."

He held it while she slipped her arms into the sleeves, then he opened the door to a car she hadn't seen before. "Whose is this?"

"Mine." He tossed her a grin. "Did you think I'd take you in the police cruiser?"

"Well, yes."

He laughed.

Oddly, the laughter eased the tension. They talked about the ranch, the orphans and Uncle Nick's health for the rest of the drive, which took almost an hour.

When he pulled into a parking area next to several buildings, she quickly checked out the crowd. People

were dressed in everything from jeans to evening outfits, but nothing too formal.

"This is the town hall." Zack gestured toward the
largest building in the complex. "It's used for meet-
ings and social functions. The library is in one end.
The brick square with the big antenna tower on top is
the sheriff's office and branch courthouse."

"Is that where you work?"

"I'm on patrol most of the time, but yes, I have a
desk in there for writing up reports, making calls and
such."

They entered the town hall. Zack hung their coats
on an empty hook mounted on the wall in an ante-
chamber before they went into the large room. Music
poured out the door. The lights were medium-low,
nice but not too intimate.

"Zack, hello. Who's this?" an attractive woman
greeted them from a table inside the door.

He handed over the tickets. "Hi, Amelia. This is
Honey Carrington. She's visiting out at the ranch.
Amelia is my landlady. She runs the best B and B in
three counties."

The woman had blue eyes and deep auburn hair
with golden highlights. Its curly masses framed her
heart-shaped face. Her smile was natural and warm.

"Welcome to Lost Valley," she said, and sounded
sincere. "Have Zack bring you over for Sunday
brunch before you leave. We serve homemade breads
and pastries made by a local woman, plus waffles and
pancakes."

"Amelia will also whip up the best omelette you ever put in your mouth," Zack informed her.

"It sounds delicious…and nonfattening, I'm sure," Honey said, ignoring the pang of envy that hit her at the admiring way Zack spoke of his landlady's abilities.

"Hey, hey, look who's here. I've been waiting for you," a male voice sang out. "You promised me a dance."

Honey recognized the young man who'd delivered the chicks. His arm was in a cast. She gave him a sympathetic smile. "Zack told me about your accident. Are you sure you're up to dancing?"

"Absolutely. Nothing keeps a good man down. The music has started. Shall we?"

A hand settled on her shoulder. "Not so fast. The first dance belongs to me," Zack declared.

Danny looked the bigger man over, then shrugged. "I'll catch you later," he murmured to her, waggled his eyebrows and was gone in the crowd.

"Young idiot," Zack muttered, but with humor.

"He's cute. And friendly."

"Like a puppy," Zack added, giving her a sexy glance that reminded her there was nothing puppylike about him.

He took her hand and guided her to the dance floor, then enfolded her in his arms, their bodies naturally melding into one as they began dancing. He lightly pressed her head to his chest, his cheek against her temple.

"Ahh, bliss." He sighed as if he'd just arrived home from a long trip.

The moment was pure fantasy, and she knew it. But it was nice to dream once in a while. For months she'd lived in fear for Adam. The past month had been one of danger for her, as well. So for this moment, she was simply a woman held sweetly in the arms of a handsome man.

The tune ended all too soon.

"Come on, let's find a seat," he suggested.

"Over here," Danny called out. He waved to the empty seats at his table. Two other guys were with him.

Zack gave a resigned shrug and escorted her over. He introduced her to Danny's friends. All three promptly claimed a dance.

"Go ahead," Zack told her. "I'll order drinks. Wine, beer or soda?"

"White wine with seltzer and lemon," she called over her shoulder as Danny led her to the crowded floor for a fast number.

By the time she'd danced with each of the others, she was ready for a break. Zack hadn't danced with anyone while she was occupied. She'd been aware of his eyes on her and of other people's eyes going from him to her as they wondered about who she was and the relationship between them.

"That was fun," she said, settling into the chair and taking a sip of the wine cooler.

"You're good. You make your partners look like

pros.'' Zack held up a glass of red wine. ''To the success of the fund-raising and the evening.''

His eyes said more, much more, causing a tremor to invade her fingers. She touched her glass to his.

When the band played a song with a cha-cha beat, Zack rose and took her to the floor again. To her surprise, he moved easily with the music, leading her into turns and twirls with aplomb.

''You've had lessons,'' she accused.

He shook his head. ''A girl I once dated taught me all I know—the waltz, fox-trot and cha-cha. We broke up before I got the tango down pat.''

At his explanation, she smiled in relief. She had no right to be jealous of his past relationships, but she couldn't deny the feeling was there.

''Maybe you can help me with that one,'' he suggested as they made their way back to the table.

''My turn,'' Danny declared, ''then I have to go. I have work to do tomorrow.''

She danced a slow number with him with a circumspect distance between them.

''So where did Zack find you?'' Danny asked. ''I haven't seen you around these parts before.''

She realized Zack could corroborate or disavow whatever she said. She tried to find a truthful path that didn't give anything away. ''We, uh, have a family connection. This is my first visit to the ranch.''

''Where are you from?''

''California originally. I love it here. The mountains are beautiful, and I'm learning to ride. Uncle Nick put me in charge of the orphan animals. I've had several learning experiences this week.''

''Such as?'' he asked.

''Hens peck when you reach under them to get an egg.''

He nodded and laughed.

''Calves want to eat all the time,'' she continued, happy to distract him from his original line of questions. ''They think I'm their mother and nearly run me over whenever I appear.''

They chatted about ranch chores for the rest of the dance. Danny said good-night and left. His friends drifted to other groups.

''Alone at last,'' Zack said with a sexy smile.

A frisson ran through her.

His voice dropped lower. ''Let's go home.''

She nodded and took the last sip of wine while he did the same. After retrieving their coats, they walked to the sporty metallic-blue car. She shivered as she slid into the cold seat.

''Here, put this around you.''

He reached over the seat and handed her the parka he'd used on the trip to the ranch. In a few minutes they were on the way home. Warm air poured from the heater.

''Thank you. That was fun,'' she said.

She glanced at him and couldn't look away. He was everything a woman could wish for in a man—handsome, steady and caring. He had sharp instincts when it came to trouble and turmoil—or maybe just when it came to her.

He stopped at an intersection before turning left onto the state road that would take them to the ranch. Catching her eye, his gaze sharpened.

"The B and B is near here," he murmured. "My room has a private entrance."

The silence arced between them, intense and urgent, as compelling as the fire now blazing in his eyes. With him, she would find sweet fulfillment.

It would be bliss. And it would be based on lies. Tomorrow always came and with it, the reckoning she'd come to expect. Then whatever they'd shared would be lost, one more thing to remember with regret....

"What troubles you so?" he asked, only slightly surprising her with the insight into her mixed emotions.

"Us," she admitted. "And all that implies."

"Which is?"

She turned from his scrutiny. The night sky stretched out into eternity, making her feel small and unimportant. She shrugged. "I don't know."

He nodded as if he understood. "Sometimes things move too fast. There are too many questions."

The questions pertained to her. She clenched her hands into fists and wished she could tell him everything—all her worries, her yearnings, her dreams.

He let off the brake and made the turn onto the road home. His home, not hers. She must remember that.

Chapter Seven

After feeding the animals Sunday morning, Honey hurried to the house to wash and change her clothes. Uncle Nick had promised them pancakes for a late breakfast. When she entered the kitchen twenty minutes later, she was surprised to see a stranger there.

"Hi," he said. "You must be Honey. Uncle Nick was just telling me about you."

The man was obviously a Dalton. His eyes were blue and his hair was brown, but not as dark as Zack's and the twins. Around six feet tall, he had the same lanky frame.

"I'm Beau Dalton," the man continued. "Coffee?"

"Yes, please. You must be one of the cousins." She took the steaming mug he poured for her.

"Beau's the doctor in the family," Uncle Nick said. He removed a towering stack of pancakes from the oven and a platter of sausages. "Put these on the table."

Honey carried the plates to the dining room.

Beau brought in two pitchers of warm syrup. "I've recently moved my office from Boise to Lost Valley."

"Do you have an office, or is it one of those mobile medical units I saw on television recently?"

"It's a regular place, located next to the post office. A nurse-practitioner works with me. She's also a midwife. Her sister-in-law is the office manager and keeps us both in line." He studied Honey for a moment. "Uncle Nick says there's a possibility you could be Tink."

She set the table with six plates. "Zack thought I could be. I have a scar on my leg. Apparently your cousin did, too. My mother died when I was three. There was also an irregularity with my birth certificate that your cousin thought was a strong point. But I really don't think three coincidences are much to go on."

"Still, they open the door to questions," he murmured.

"Yes. There are questions."

The front door opened. Zack and the twins entered. They called out jovial greetings to their cousin.

During the meal, she learned that Beau's sister, the female cousin, lived in Boise. She worked on software learning programs for elementary schools, but wanted to start her own business. The city had a booming technology industry and the economy was growing, according to Beau.

"I'm thinking of buying a house here," Beau confided, "before land prices go up."

"Are you expecting a land boom up here?" Zack asked, openly amused.

Beau grinned, but his answer was serious. "It could happen. Lots of folks are looking for second homes. With the lake and mountains, plus the peace and quiet, this would be a nice place to bring the family."

"You thinking of marrying?" Uncle Nick asked, his eyes brightening with approval.

"Who would want someone who works all the time, even if he does become embarrassingly rich?" Trevor wanted to know.

Beau ignored his cousin. "Sorry, Uncle, no bride in the offing. I'm just following Seth's advice about investments and all."

"Seth is the lawyer cousin," Zack explained to her. "He does everyone's taxes and manages the ranch books. He also scolds us about our finances."

"Or lack thereof," Trevor added a trifle gloomily.

"Don't forget to show up at the office for your checkup tomorrow," Beau warned Uncle Nick. "Ten o'clock sharp."

"I'll remember." The uncle peered at Honey. "Can you drive me in after the chores are done?"

"Of course." She was both flattered and flustered to be given the task. A flush rose to her face when she

Play the
Lucky
He[art]

and get...

2 FREE BOO[KS]

and a **FREE MYST[ERY GIFT]**

yes! YOURS [...]

I have scratched off t[he...]
Please send me my *2 FREE [BOOKS and a]*
FREE Mystery GIFT. I underst[and I am]
under no obligation to purchase [anything,]
explained on the back of this card[.]

335 SDL DUZW

FIRST NAME		LA[ST NAME]
ADDRESS		
APT.#	CITY	
STATE/PROV.	ZIP/POSTAL [CODE]	

Twenty-one gets you
2 FREE BOOKS
and a **FREE MYSTERY GIFT!**

Twenty gets y[ou]
2 FREE BOO[KS]

Offer limited to one per household and n[ot valid to current]
subscribers. All orders subject to approva[l.]

▼ *Silhouette*®
Where love comes alive™

Visit us online at
www.eHarlequin.com

The Silhouette Reader Service™ — Here's how it works:

If offer card is missing write to: The Silhouette Reader Service, 3010 Walden Ave., P.O. Box 1867, Buffalo, NY 14240-1867

BUSINESS REPLY MAIL
FIRST-CLASS MAIL   PERMIT NO. 717-003   BUFFALO, NY

POSTAGE WILL BE PAID BY ADDRESSEE

SILHOUETTE READER SERVICE
3010 WALDEN AVE
PO BOX 1867
BUFFALO NY 14240-9952

NO POSTAGE
NECESSARY
IF MAILED
IN THE
UNITED STATES

realized all the Dalton men were gazing at her, mostly with pleased expressions.

Except Zack.

She couldn't tell what he was thinking. A mask had been drawn over his emotions during the night. This morning he'd seemed to distance himself as he joined the twins in doing the outside chores. He'd observed her with the orphans but hadn't offered help or suggestions.

"Tomorrow," she repeated. "At ten."

"Then we'll have lunch in town. You want to join us?" Uncle Nick asked Beau.

Beau shook his head. "No time. I'll grab a sandwich at my desk between patients." He glanced at his cousins. "The valley is growing, population-wise. I think there're going to be business opportunities opening up. You guys should think about starting a resort."

"Yeah? After we rob the branch bank?" Trevor asked.

His cousin grinned. "Seth and I might be able to help in the financial department."

"I'm not having a bunch of tourists cluttering up the ranch," Uncle Nick stated firmly.

Beau agreed. "I was thinking of a place on Lost Valley reservoir. The lake is a popular fishing hole. It can be used for recreation such as swimming, water-skiing and kayaking. Amelia may be interested. She said something about expanding recently."

Honey realized he meant the woman she'd met last night, the gorgeous redhead who ran the bed-and-breakfast where Zack stayed. Were the cousins competing for the woman's affections? Not that it was any of her business.

"Good thinking, cuz," Zack chimed in. "Amelia would know how to run things. We could have a first-class restaurant on the lake, a store for supplies, groceries and gifts, maybe some cabins, along with a lodge. Heck, we can build all those ourselves."

"And cut the timber here," Beau added.

As Honey listened to the men plot the steps that would lead to this vacation paradise, she tried to ignore an increasing sense of isolation. She hadn't heard from her brother at all during the week she'd been at the ranch. He hadn't answered her e-mail.

No news was probably good news in this case.

Hearing a calf bawl in the pasture, she realized the week had passed quickly, yet she felt she'd been here forever, as if this was her home and she'd returned after a long and arduous journey through a perilous world.

"What do you think?" Zack asked her.

She stared at him blankly.

"You weren't listening," he accused.

"Well, I was, then my mind went off on a tangent as I considered the attractions of the area. People from Boise would probably love to be able to come up here for weekends and vacations. It would be very convenient."

"See?" Beau demanded. "It's a good idea."

Uncle Nick snorted. "Have you run this by Seth?"

Seth was obviously the business guru of the family. Honey had no doubt about the cousins succeeding in any endeavor they tried. They seemed to function as a team.

"He agrees the idea has possibilities," Beau said. "We should start looking for the right property."

The men discussed the Lost Valley area thoroughly during the meal and the rest of the morning. That afternoon they had popcorn and soda while watching a basketball game on TV. Honey excused herself and went to the rose bedroom.

She checked her e-mails again. Still finding none from Adam, she decided to send one to him asking that he call her at the ranch on her cell phone as soon as she could.

She just had to talk to him, to hear his voice and know he was okay. Most of all, she wanted to leave. Each day drew her more deeply into the lives of the Daltons. Each day the lonely need to…to *belong* grew stronger.

After sending the e-mail, she sat in front of the blank screen, lost in thought. She was nearly twenty-six, but she felt much older. A wish for permanence, someplace to call her own, assailed her. Certainly her aunt's house had never been home for two orphans with nowhere to go, but here…here the contentment oozed from the land, filling her with a yearning for something different in her life. She couldn't even say what that something was.

Restless, she deleted her copy of the e-mail, shut

down the computer and went outside. Walking along
the path to the back of the house, she found a swing
attached to a tree limb. The sun shone warmly on the
spot. Sitting there, she swung idly back and forth while
gazing at the mountains, her mind on the future.

She'd thought she would stay with the dance company for a few years, save her money and open her
own dance school. That had been her personal goal.

Idly she wondered if Lost Valley and the surround-
ing area could support such a thing. She could check
on the number of schoolchildren in the area. There
might be enough to support year-round classes. Adam
had said he would help with the finances.

With a sigh, she rose and walked along a tiny creek
that burbled behind the house. Uncle Nick had said it
was seasonal, running in the spring due to snowmelt
and in the summer due to storms. Like her, it was only
a temporary thing in this wild, fascinating landscape.

Zack knocked softly on Honey's door. No answer.
He tried again. She must be sleeping. He debated the
wisdom of waking her. Wasn't there some old adage
about letting sleeping dogs lie?

Smiling, he knocked harder, then opened the door
and called her name. Still no answer. He realized the
room was empty. Going inside, he quickly checked
just to be sure she was gone. Her coat and the jacket
he'd given her were lying on a chair, so she hadn't
gone far.

He peered out the front windows, but didn't see her. Crossing to the back wall, he surveyed the yard and got a glimpse of movement along the creek. She was out for a walk, heading up the slope.

Gauging the position of the sun, he wondered if she realized how late it was. Uncle Nick wanted the chores done early tonight so they could finish in the kitchen before his favorite crime show on the tube.

Zack noticed the laptop on the writing table. He wondered who she corresponded with. With a grimace, he realized he was more than merely curious. He wanted to know things about her—her favorite color, the funniest thing that had ever happened to her, the scariest, the best...

He stopped as a mix of emotions rose in him, the only sound that of his heart, beating fast and irregularly.

Anything permanent with Honey was out of the question. She'd made that clear. If he couldn't trust a woman he'd known all his life, what made him think things would be different with a mysterious woman he'd just met?

He realized he was definitely not seeing her in a cousinly light. Frowning, he left the room, his mood dark and confused.

He declined a game of cards with Beau and the twins and headed for his room. He wondered if the detective from Vegas had any information to offer about their mysterious and beguiling guest.

* * *

Honey noticed that Zack spent most of Monday and Tuesday in town. When he was at the ranch, he stayed out in the pastures, working with his horses.

She, too, was busy. After returning from Beau's office with Uncle Nick, she began the transition of the orphans to the fields with the other herd animals of their kind under the old man's direction.

In the afternoon, she read ranching magazines from cover to cover. On Tuesday, over the evening meal, she asked a hundred questions when all of them sat down at the table together. Zack said little, but the twins willingly took part in her education.

"It's time you started riding every day," Trevor declared after dinner on Tuesday evening. "That's the only way to toughen up."

"She doesn't need to toughen up," Zack said. "She'll be leaving at the end of the month."

An uncomfortable silence ensued at his statement, although its tone was matter-of-fact.

"I've enjoyed learning about the animals," Honey told him, unable to keep the defensive note hidden.

"What about your career?"

She managed to smile. "Being a waitress isn't all that much of a career."

"I meant your dancing."

"Oh, that." She hesitated, then spoke truthfully. "I'd really like to open my own dance school someday, maybe in Lost Valley."

Four pairs of identical blue eyes observed her with varying degrees of interest.

Flustered, she added, "I mean, in a small town such as Lost Valley, someplace quiet and safe and—"

"Safe?" Zack questioned.

"A place where people know each other. Not like Los Angeles or Las Vegas where everyone's a stranger."

Uncle Nick gave his approval. "That sounds like a wise plan. Lost Valley needs more activities for its young folks."

Trevor assumed a deadpan expression. "I agree. All the guys I know will be lining up for a chance to jump around a stage in a tutu."

The three brothers broke into laughter as Uncle Nick gave them a look of disgust.

Honey smiled at Trevor. "Guys do need lessons in modern and ballroom dances so they're more at ease on the dance floor. It's a pleasure to partner with someone who's really good."

"Like you," Trevor said. "Danny was impressed with your ability. 'Like dancing with an angel' was his comment."

"Is Lost Valley big enough to support a dance school?" Zack asked.

"I don't know," she admitted. "That's something I would have to investigate."

"Seth could help you," Travis said in his quiet, thoughtful manner.

Trevor agreed. "Seth knows everything."

Zack gave a low snort. When the twins peered at

him, he stared back without saying anything. The twins grinned.

Honey didn't have time to assess the byplay between the brothers. Her mind was off on its own wild scheme.

Actually she had saved quite a bit of money since she'd begun dancing. She'd thought to retire from the stage when she was thirty-five, if all went well, and open her school in some small town along the California coast. Idaho would do just as well.

"That Amelia is a smart woman," Uncle Nick told her. He glanced at Zack. "You could ask her what she thinks about the dance school. She might know a place Honey could use."

Honey ignored the disturbing pang that went through her at the mention of Zack's landlady. "Thank you," she said sincerely. "It probably won't pan out, but this is a wonderful place to live."

She lost her train of thought at Zack's narrow-eyed scrutiny. A buzz interrupted the tense atmosphere.

Zack glanced at the pager on his belt. "The dispatcher," he said. "I'll have to call in."

No one said anything when he went to his bedroom and returned the call. In a couple of minutes he emerged. He wore a gun strapped to his waist and carried a jacket and another item in his hand.

"What's happened?" Uncle Nick asked.

"Robbery at the gas-station market. The clerk was shot."

"How bad is he hurt?"

"Critical. I've got to go."

"Do you need the volunteer deputies?" Travis asked.

"Not yet. Dispatch will call if we do."

The twins nodded.

Honey's chest was so tight she could scarcely pull air into her lungs as she and the family watched Zack race off down the ranch road toward the small town that had seemed so safe to her.

No place was totally safe and secure, she reflected. Bad things happened everywhere. Anyone could be attacked, as the clerk had been. Zack could be shot, too.

With a start, she realized he'd thought of that. The other item he'd carried with him had been a bullet-proof vest.

At three in the morning—it was now Wednesday— Honey peered out the window into the night once more. No headlights broke the line of darkness stretching toward town. She paced the length of the bedroom and wondered if Zack and the other deputies had caught the robber.

Unable to lie in bed, she wandered down the hall to the kitchen where a dim light cast an eerie glow. Maybe a cup of cocoa would help.

She poured milk into a cup, then hesitated. At that moment she picked up a low vibration on the air. Rushing to the living room, she saw lights on the road.

With a lightness that made her dizzy, she returned

to the kitchen, filled a second cup, added cocoa mix to both containers and placed them in the microwave to heat. They were ready when Zack entered the house and came to the kitchen door.

"Hi," she said softly. "I've made cocoa. I thought you might like a cup when you got in." When he didn't respond, she stopped in uncertainty. "Did you get the robber?" she finally asked.

He tossed his jacket and the vest on a chair. "Yeah, we got him." He took a seat at the table.

"Good." She noted the fatigue on his face as she placed the mug of steaming cocoa on the table. She quickly sat in her usual chair and sipped the hot drink before she did something stupid, such as brush the wave back from his brow and cradle his head against her.

The silence thickened until it felt like a dense screen between them. She decided to finish up and go to her room—where she should have stayed in the first place. She'd never felt so unwelcome as she did at this moment.

He took a long swallow of the cocoa. When he set the mug down, she saw it was nearly empty. He sighed and rubbed a hand over his face.

"You're tired. Go to bed," she encouraged. "I'll put the mugs in the dishwasher."

He downed the last sip, then stood.

She did the same, then rinsed the cups and tucked them into the dishwasher rack. Zack watched from the doorway.

When she went to the door, he didn't move. She stopped in front of him and studied his face. His eyes were dark and he seemed filled with thoughts she couldn't read.

"Well," she said. She inhaled slowly and caught a faint whiff of his cologne and talc. Longing drowned her sense of self-preservation as she gazed at him. "What is it?" she asked, sensing more than fatigue in him.

He shook his head. "Nothing."

She knew that was a lie. "What happened tonight?"

The silence lasted a full ten seconds, then, "I might have killed a man," he said.

"The robber?"

"Yes."

"How?"

"We set up a roadblock. He crashed through it. I shot out his back tires. He lost control, veered off the road and crashed into a ravine."

"Did a bullet hit him?"

"No. I don't think so. But he's in critical condition and may not live."

She didn't say anything for a long time. When she spoke, she did so thoughtfully. "He chose to rob the market. He chose to injure another person. He chose to run the roadblock. We all have to take responsibility for our decisions, the good and the bad."

"I knew what I was doing," he told her. "I acted deliberately, knowing I could cause another person bodily harm to the point of loss of life. At one point, I think I even wanted him dead.''

"Will the clerk from the market live?'' Honey asked.

"I don't know.''

"Then we'll have to wait. You did the best you could. It's in the hands of God now.''

Zack pressed his face into her hair, then kissed her on the temple, filled with emotions too tumultuous, too complicated, to define. He wanted only to hold his woman and let the peace she'd given him drive everything else from his mind.

His woman?

This woman, he corrected. He meant this woman. Looking into her concerned eyes, he saw all the things that made a man want to come home to someone…someone special…someone just for him….

Honey barely had time to gasp in surprise before his lips closed over hers. The kiss was demanding, desperate and oddly tender, as if he poured his soul into it.

For the briefest instant, she worried about the wisdom of a kiss, then it was gone. A tiny glow began within her, radiating warmth and joy and all the things she knew weren't real. But she wanted them. She wanted them!

He made a sound, a raw moan of longing deep in his throat. Forgetting a lifetime of caution, she wrapped her arms tightly around his shoulders and let herself cling to his solid form.

A shudder went through him. "Need you," he whispered. "God, I need you. For the last hour, all I could think of was home and *you*."

"Yes," she said, leaning her head back as he burned kisses along her throat. "Oh, yes."

He lifted her as if she weighed nearly nothing and carried her to the bedroom at the end of the west wing. When he set her on her feet beside the rose-covered bedspread, he lifted her chin and stared into her eyes as if looking for something elusive but important.

She held his gaze and let him look into her soul, open now as she'd never allowed herself to be in the past. With him, she had no secrets, no doubts, no fears.

"It's all right," she heard herself say and hadn't any idea what she meant.

"Is it?" he questioned with a trace of deep sadness. "Make it that way," he said, giving her a haunted look.

She pushed the lock of hair off his forehead. "I will," she promised. "I will."

After tossing her robe aside, she went to work on his buttons. Soon they were both undressed, their breaths coming in shallow pants as they gazed at each other.

His skin was darker than hers with a distinct line at the waist, the result of going without a shirt during the hot summer days. His chest was lightly furred with a patch of black hair in a rough diamond shape.

She rubbed her hand over it, finding a deep pleasure in the tactile sensation. Beneath the wiry covering, she felt the warmth radiating from his skin. Dipping her head, she kissed him in the center of his chest, then over to each side.

Putting her hands on his waist, she stretched up on her toes and planted kisses along his jaw, then leaned into him so that his erection pressed intimately against her abdomen. She brushed slowly from side to side.

He closed his eyes and caught her against his strong frame. ''You feel good,'' he whispered, burying his face in her hair. ''You don't know how good.''

''Show me,'' she invited, surer of herself as the passion grew. It had to come to this between them, she thought in a second of clarity before her mind was enclosed in the hazy crimson of desire.

He urged her down on the bed, in the place she'd tried to sleep before rising to wait for his return. When he joined her, lying beside her so that they touched from chest to toes, she welcomed him into her embrace.

''Let me look at you,'' he said huskily, his voice softer now as fatigue and regret faded into the background.

She raised heavy eyelids and returned his gaze. Along with a touching sadness at what he'd had to do that night, she witnessed other emotions in him. He touched her with great tenderness. She hugged him close.

Bending his head, he took her mouth in a kiss that sent her senses spinning out of control. The danger to her heart, to trusting someone, to needing another person, disappeared in the whirlwind of ecstasy that filled her to overflowing.

He caressed every nook and cranny of her until she gasped with pleasure and the hunger he induced.

She did the same to him, finding the sensitive places, the full masculine beauty that was his. She reveled in his self-control even as she experienced the great strength of his body, his muscles like steel as he moved gently against her, inciting them both to raging hunger.

"Please," she whispered at one point. "I need you. I need you now...."

Zack kissed her eyes, her nose, the corners of her mouth. "You don't know what need is, how I felt when I came in and realized you were awake...that you'd waited for me. It was..." He shook his head, unable to find words.

"I know," she said, driving him crazy with her sweet light touches. "I do know."

"No, you have no idea," he insisted.

He took her mouth in greedy delight, the hunger so strong he was afraid he'd hurt her. Clamping down on the desire, he caressed her intimately until she writhed under him and demanded that he come to her. At last, he had no choice. He rose over her, then moved away.

"Wait," he said. "I have protection."

She waited, her hands restless on his body as he prepared for her, glad to do this, to protect her as much as he could from the need that drove them both.

He looked into her eyes. There was acceptance

there, as if she'd known for some time that this moment was inevitable. And there was more. Trust, he realized. There was trust in that clear gaze.

Something inside him seemed to swell, then burst open in a gentle outpouring, like spring rain blowing softly over the parched winter land. Still staring into her eyes, he positioned himself and slowly, carefully entered her in a shower of bliss that made him feel humble, almost reverent.

"Move in me," she whispered. "Now."

At her passionate urging, he gave up further attempts at control. It was impossible. He let himself blend into her, become part of her—breath of her breath, heart of her heart, blood surging and ebbing in one tidal wave of desperate hunger.

Against all reason, he needed her. This woman. This one. None other.

Honey felt the tension gathering in her. From a distance she heard her own voice, the little sighs and moans of passion nearing its climax. He was the most generous of lovers, mindful of her and her needs, gently urging her to take from him, holding back his own wild hunger until she was ready.

And then she was.

She cried out as wave after wave of fulfillment washed over her. As she did, he let himself go over the crest, too.

The afterglow left her exhausted but peaceful.

He lay beside her for a long time, neither of them

moving except for a grateful caress with fingertips once in a while.

"Shall I go?" he at last asked as they heard the living-room clock strike the hour just before dawn.

"No."

He sighed and snuggled his cheek into her hair. "Good," he whispered, and kissed her ear. "Because I don't think I could."

She lay there in his arms and listened to the quiet, peaceful sound of his breathing. A haven, she thought.

Peace and quiet and safety, he'd promised.

She'd found them all.

But had she lost her heart?

Chapter Eight

It was almost eleven by the time Honey awoke. Zack stood beside the bed, dressed in fresh clothing, his hair still damp from a shower. She watched him, not sure what to say.

He smiled slightly. "I'm heading for the office," he told her. "I want to check on the clerk and the guy who robbed him. I'm heading the robbery investigation and may not be able to get back to the ranch tonight."

She nodded.

He hesitated, then bent and gave her a swift kiss. After he left, she rose, bathed and dressed, aware of a slight stiffness as she moved. Last night had been foolish, and Zack was right to put distance between them.

There was no time for the complexities of an involvement. As soon as she heard from Adam, she would leave.

Yes, that was the sensible thing to do, she repeated silently over and over as she went into the kitchen. Zack's uncle was there, removing a package from the freezer.

"The orphans," she said, remembering them for the first time. "They haven't had breakfast."

Uncle Nick peered at her from under his shaggy eyebrows. "The boys fed them, so there's no need to worry."

"They were my responsibility and I forgot all about them until just now. That makes me feel terrible."

"You needed to rest. I made a pot of fresh coffee if you want some."

Heat rose to her face as she met his gaze. She saw only kindness and patience there. Turning abruptly, she poured a cup of coffee, then gazed out the windows at the mountains.

A shaky sigh escaped her. She had to get away from the ranch. It was too dangerous for reasons that had nothing to do with the men who were after her brother. She was growing attached to the place.

And to the Daltons?

Yes, she admitted, careful not to single out any particular one. She'd come to care for them and that was the most dangerous thing of all. She knew better than to let herself need anyone.

"It's time to change the older laying hens to corn,"

Uncle Nick said, breaking into her introspection, "the ones that have about quit laying."

Forcing her mind to practical matters, she asked, "Why do we do that?"

"It makes them taste better."

That stumped her, but only for a second. "Are you going to eat them?" she said incredulously.

He nodded toward the chicken he'd unwrapped from the freezer paper. "We freeze them until we need them." He gave her a sharp perusal. "Are you one of those people who thinks meat comes prepackaged and frozen without going through the processes of growth and marketing?"

"No, but I never thought the hens would become Sunday dinner."

"We don't run an old-age home for chickens," he told her, his manner humorous but gentle, as if he understood her dismay.

She managed a smile. "Of course not. I hadn't really thought it out, that's all." She eyed the chicken he was preparing for the oven, which would be served at supper that night. There were lots of things she hadn't really thought out regarding her visit to the ranch. For instance, she'd never considered the possibility of falling in love.

Not that she had, but it could happen.

Zack found he had an e-mail from the Vegas detective. The lawman told him to call when he had a moment. He grabbed the phone and punched in the number. The detective answered on the second ring.

"Zack Dalton here," he said. "Do you have any information on Hannah Carrington?"

"I think so. I found a dance troupe that had one of its star members quit a little over a month ago and disappear from sight. That's around the same time Bert said the new girl started working as a waitress."

"Right."

"The troupe didn't fold, though. It has a contract until the end of the year with the casino. And the woman's name wasn't Carrington, although she fits the description you gave me."

Zack's worry grew. What had she gotten herself involved in? Dammit, he'd get the truth out of her one way or another. "What name did she use as a dancer?"

"Hannah Smith. She was blue-eyed and a natural blonde, according to the business manager. Her nickname was Honey."

"At least that's consistent," Zack muttered.

"There was a man in her life. A couple of times on a cell phone she talked to a man she called Adam, but no one ever saw him. One of the dancers thought Smith had met him on the Internet because she was always checking her e-mails on a laptop."

"Another piece that checks out," Zack said. "I've seen the laptop."

"She's from Los Angeles and was raised by an aunt. The aunt's name is—wait, I have it written down somewhere—ah, Carrington. Elaine Carrington. She was listed as the emergency contact for Smith. That's all I've been able to come up with.''

''That's more than I had a day ago,'' Zack told the detective. ''Thanks. I owe you.''

After hanging up, he considered the evidence. It all pointed to one thing—Hannah Carrington, alias Hannah Smith, also known as Honey, was in trouble or she wouldn't be using different names. Now all he had to do was find out what kind of trouble. And how it affected his family.

Damn, but things were complicated. Last night should never have happened. Desire messed with a man's mind, and he'd certainly been in a daze during the hours in her arms. A really stupid thing to do.

But he couldn't find it in himself to regret it.

Muttering an expletive, he picked up the phone again and called the hospital in Boise. Both the clerk and the robber were alive and out of danger. No one was going to die because of him. He wished his other problems would clear up so easily.

Actually there was just one problem. Honey. It was one he meant to solve.

Honey brought the calves into the pen and fed them before doing the same for the lambs, then the two colts. After shooing them back into the pasture, she checked on the dozen laying hens.

She found two eggs, one of them under the biddy who always tried to peck her. ''I hope you go into the roasting pot first,'' she muttered while the hen pecked furiously at Honey's hand as she pulled the egg out of the nest.

As she filled the feeders, she considered her attitude toward the old hen. Because that particular hen was a pain, she wasn't horrified by its fate. In fact, she was downright vengeful. How personal everything becomes, she mused, observing the other nesting chickens.

Her thoughts immediately reverted to the previous night. Zack had been the most wonderful of lovers— gentle but demanding, considerate of her pleasure and desires. She'd never felt so cherished. He'd needed her, and for those few hours, she'd let herself need him.

Don't, she warned her heart. Don't fall in love. Don't yearn. Don't dream. Don't breathe, she ended, reaching inside for the cynicism that had sustained her in the past, but finding only an aching sadness. Nothing real could happen between them. It just wasn't possible.

The chores finished, she returned to the house and went to her room. She wanted to check her e-mails. Nothing.

After a futile period of worrying about her brother, she turned her thoughts to Zack and waited for him to come home.

But midnight came and went without his appearance at the homestead. So apparently he *had* decided to spend the night in town. She went to bed but not to sleep. Her mind churned endlessly as the need to tell Zack the truth grew within her. She had to talk to Adam first, but maintaining a lie was becoming more and more difficult.

As it turned out, she needn't have worried. Zack didn't return to the ranch for days. On Sunday Honey went for a long walk along the creek. A police cruiser was parked in front of the porch when she returned. Uncle Nick and the twins had gone to church while she'd elected to stay at the ranch and thus out of sight.

Knowing Zack was inside and that they would be there alone, she hesitated at the door.

"I wondered if you were going to come in," he said when she finally did enter. His tone was somewhat teasing, but his eyes were serious. A premonition of trouble came to her.

Her heart pounded like a death knell. She hung the hat and jacket he'd lent her on a hook and smoothed her hair back from her face while ignoring the remark. "The wind is strong today. There's a storm approaching, I understand."

"Maybe more than one," he said with a certain edge to the words, his voice harder.

He was seated in the leather recliner, his long legs stretched out and crossed at the ankles. His jeans and white shirt looked crisp and freshly ironed, as if they'd just come back from the laundry.

"What's the other one?" she asked, sure it pertained to her, judging by the piercing study he made of her.

"You."

She perched on the arm of the sofa and kept her face expressionless the way she'd learned to do when her aunt accused her of something she hadn't done. "What offense have I committed, or doesn't the prisoner get to know?"

He pushed the wave of hair off his forehead, his action indicating reluctance to broach whatever was bothering him. When he spoke, he was blunt. "Who are you?"

The suddenness of the question caused her to start. For a second she couldn't think. "Who wants to know?"

"I do."

"Why?"

He looked as if he would like to choke the information out of her. She returned his hard stare with an insouciant lift of her brows, reverting instinctively to actions learned long ago to conceal emotion.

Her nerves leaped when he stood and in two strides was beside her. He lifted a lock of her hair and studied it intently. "Your hair is naturally blond," he said. "Why the dark roots?"

"I thought it went with the waitressing outfit."

That brought him up short, then he frowned. "Why?" he repeated very, very softly.

He stood close, close enough that she could feel his heat along her thigh and hip. The closeness made it harder to think. For a terrible moment she wanted to lean into him and rest, letting his strength absorb her worries.

She moved her head, dislodging the curl from his loose clasp. "Have you been checking on me?"

"Yes."

"Why?" she demanded, tossing the question back to him.

"I wanted to know what you were hiding."

She clasped her hands in her lap. "Find anything interesting?" she challenged, and hated the defensive note in her voice. It was how she'd responded to her aunt and sounded childish.

"Yes."

His tone was cool. She remembered last Sunday night when it had been warm. Warm and husky and caring. She blanked out the memory and said nothing.

"Does the name Hannah Smith mean anything to you?" he asked after a full minute of silence.

"It's my name. Hannah Amity Smith, after my grandmother and my mother's best friend. But I've always been called Honey as long as I can remember."

"So you admit you've been using a false name," he said, again in a soft voice that sounded all the more dangerous for its lack of expression.

"I used my aunt's last name, yes."

"Why?" he asked again.

She wondered where Adam was and why he hadn't called. She needed desperately to know what she should do. How could it hurt to tell Zack the truth?

He was a law officer. And Uncle Nick would never betray her whereabouts. With a defeated sigh, she admitted she trusted them completely.

"There are some men looking for me. I don't know who they are, but they want to know where someone is, someone I know," she added before he could ask who and why.

"Such as Adam?"

Her hands jerked before she could control them. He glanced down, then back to her face.

"Yes." She inhaled carefully, knowing denial was useless. "He's an agent with the FBI. His cover was blown while following a drug and money-laundering trail that led to the police. The enforcers are looking for him."

A quick glance assured her that Zack knew what an enforcer's duty was.

"What's your part in all this?"

"Adam says they want to use me to get to him."

Zack inhaled sharply. "Is he your lover?"

She hesitated, hurt by his suspicion that she would take a second lover while involved with another. "He's my brother."

"Brother?" Zack repeated as if it was a foreign word. "He's your brother?"

"Adam is my brother," she affirmed, a fierceness coming over her as she stood, forcing him to step back. "He's my real family, my only family. He was always there for me when I needed him. I would do anything for him."

"Including give up your career and lie to cover your tracks," he concluded.

"Yes." She maintained the defiant stance for another second, then moved away from him. "If these men should find me... They won't hesitate to use force on me, to get information about my brother." She gave Zack an apologetic glance. "I've been worried about your family. Uncle Nick is one of a kind."

Zack recognized the guilt he'd seen before in her. An odd tightness in his chest eased. She had a conscience. She was concerned about his family. The other man in her life was her brother. He got the picture.

"But," she continued a trifle anxiously, "I really don't think anyone will find me in Idaho. After all, it is sort of the back of beyond."

The rueful little smile that curved her lips touched him in ways he didn't have time to think about at present.

"Yeah, I agree," he said on a lighter note. Her story clicked with all he'd learned. "Okay, most of the pieces fit now, so I'm going to believe your story."

"Thanks."

He heaved a deep breath. "Okay, okay, I do believe you." He tipped her chin up and gazed into the light-blue eyes that could hide so much—and promise the world.

"So where do we go from here?" she asked, meeting his gaze levelly.

She was brave. He had to give her that. "I'm not

sure. This is Uncle Nick's home. We'll need to talk to him.''

''Yes, you're right. I'll tell him everything as soon as he gets back.''

Zack nodded, not sure whether he felt relief, anger or, even weirder, hope. He hated lies and subterfuge and she'd come clean about her reasons for being here. That was a start, but of what?

A future for them? some part deep inside suggested.

He didn't have time to think about that right now. There were other problems to be considered.

''I'd like to go to my room for a while.'' She walked away, her head bowed as if she was deep in thought.

He watched her leave, her movements graceful, as lithe as a mountain cat. The blood pounded insistently through him, reminding him of other ways she pleased him.

Where do we go from here?

Her question pounded in his brain. He wished he knew.

Honey surveyed the lovely rose bedroom, including the closet. She didn't see any forgotten items. Her bags were packed and ready to go. She'd checked the laptop once more and found no messages from Adam.

Heaviness sat on her shoulders that no amount of reason could dispel. She didn't want to leave.

There, she'd admitted it. Not that her wants or

wishes made any difference at all in the grand scheme of things. She sighed and headed for the living room.

Uncle Nick and the twins had returned. The twins were at the stables, so only Zack and his uncle were at the house. It was confession time.

Two pairs of blue eyes gazed solemnly at her when she entered the comfortable room. She sat on a hassock, folded her hands together and, looking at the older man, began.

"Has Zack told you my life story?" she asked, managing a wry smile.

"Some of it," Uncle Nick said. "I had a feeling there was more to you than met the eye."

She stared at her clasped hands. "I didn't like deceiving you. It was just that I needed to get away."

Uncle Nick nodded. "So you could protect your brother. It was a wise thing to do."

Her head jerked up. She stared at him and saw only concern and kindness. A hot ache settled behind her eyes, misting her vision. She blinked rapidly.

"I could have put your family in danger. I hope you will forgive me for that. I don't think anyone has followed me or knows—" She stopped and gave Zack a worried frown as realization dawned on her. "Who did you ask about me? How did you find out my name and that of my aunt?"

"A detective I worked with in Vegas."

"Did he check with the Los Angeles police? If he did, do you know who he talked to?" she demanded as new fears arose.

"He talked to Bert at the casino and a couple of people with the dance company. I don't know who else."

"Someone in the L.A. Internal Affairs Department leaked my brother's cover," she explained. "Adam told me not to trust any cops until this job was finished." She stopped and stared at Zack.

"Now they might know to come here to look for you if they trace the Vegas detective's inquiries back to me," he said, voicing her fears.

"Yes." She leaped to her feet, already feeling the hot breath of the enforcers down her neck. "This might bring the men directly to your door. I'll leave right away."

Uncle Nick held up a hand. "Let's don't go off half-cocked. We need to think this through."

Honey shook her head. "Zack can take me to the bus station in Boise. I'll go someplace…to Chicago or someplace big where it's easy to get lost."

Zack rose from the leather recliner and towered over her. "You won't go anywhere," he said in a low tone.

"I have to."

"Zack's right," Uncle Nick interrupted the beginning quarrel. "You need to stay here where it's safe."

"No place is safe," she said in a choked voice, the heaviness becoming a hard, aching knot in her chest.

Zack laid a hand on her shoulder. "Do you think we'll let anyone harm you?" he asked, his manner protective.

Warmth eased her ache a tiny bit as she gazed into

his eyes. She laid a hand on his chest and felt the steady beat of his heart. "I can't put you and your family at greater risk."

He returned to his usual endearingly, arrogantly masculine ways. "You have no choice."

She lifted her chin. "You're right. I have to leave."

"Dammit, Honey, that's not what I meant. You have to stay here. For your brother's sake."

This made no sense to her. "It's for his that I came here. It's for him that I have to leave. And for everyone else," she added. "Your family has been wonderful. I really can't—"

"Yes, you can," Zack informed her. "You agreed to stay until the end of the month. That was the deal. You either stay willingly or by force. Take your pick."

She stood toe-to-toe with him. "You can't force me to stay."

"Yes, he can," Uncle Nick calmly joined in the fray. "The twins will help. So will I."

She looked from one set of implacable blue eyes to the other. "You are the most stubborn family I have ever met," she told them, furious and frustrated and despairing of pounding sense into their thick heads. "The whole bunch of you are so gullible it's pitiful. Anyone could take you in with a sob story."

Uncle Nick laughed as if she'd said something really funny. Zack chuckled, too.

"Well," he drawled, "we've sometimes accused each other of being boneheaded and stupid, so to me, stubborn and gullible seem pretty mild as far as insults go. Don't they to you, Uncle Nick?''

The older man agreed, then sobered. ''I think you should listen to Zack. You're safer here with the boys to watch out for any bad guys that might show up. Your brother knows where you are so he can concentrate on his job without worrying too much about you. And—'' he added the clincher ''—Zack and I will be able to sleep at night, knowing that you're under our roof.''

Zack nodded adamantly. His expression softened as he leaned close to her. ''So you'll stay?''

Honey pressed a hand to her chest, holding in emotions that threatened to get out of control. She tried to think, to be wise and clear-sighted, but it was impossible.

''I'll stay,'' she finally said, feeling terribly humble and grateful for their protective concern. ''For now.''

Flames seemed to dance in Zack's eyes as he smiled approval at her, then turned to his uncle. ''We need a plan. Honey isn't to be left alone at any time.''

''Right. One of the twins can work near the house until we hear from Honey's brother. Adam is his name?'' Uncle Nick asked her. At her nod, he continued planning aloud. ''If she needs to go to town, someone will go with her.''

''I'll stay out here,'' Zack said. ''I'll alert everyone at the office to be on the lookout for strangers, especially if they start asking about Honey.'' He turned to her. "We know every man and woman on the force here. You'll be safe."

"That's settled then," the older man stated. "Call the twins in. Dinner should be about ready."

As Honey put out plates and silverware, then helped set Sunday dinner on the table, she realized how *normal* it all seemed. The Daltons got on with life, no matter what.

She heard Zack give a holler out the front door. In a few minutes the twins entered the living room. They hung up their hats, then pulled off their boots, placed them neatly in a row by the wall and filed into the dining room after washing up at the kitchen sink.

"Something smells good," Trevor said. "I'm starved."

"Roast chicken," Travis guessed, sniffing the air.

Uncle Nick placed the platter of meat, surrounded by carrots and potatoes and onions, in the center of the big table. "We'll say grace. Thank you, Lord, for bringing Honey to us and for giving us multiple blessings of family and friends. Help us be strong in times of trouble and always be thankful for our daily bread. Amen."

After the prayer, Trevor peered across the table at her. "Is there something going on that we should know about?"

A hand touched hers under cover of the table and squeezed gently. Zack gave her a smile that made her heart thump loudly when she looked at him.

"I'd like to introduce you to our guest," he said to

the twins. "Her name is Hannah Smith, and she has a story to tell us."

At his encouraging nod, she told them about her brother and her reasons for coming to the ranch.

"So you're not our cousin," Trevor concluded. He looked at his older brother and back at her.

Honey felt her face grow warm. Suddenly a world of possibilities opened before her—safety, friends, family, a home. Everything seemed possible. The Dalton confidence had infected her, too.

Chapter Nine

The following morning Honey finished her chores quickly, then approached Zack as he came out of the stable enclosure leading a sturdy cow pony. "I need to go to town for some things," she told him.

He nodded. "We can go around noon. I need to exercise Caesar first. You want to saddle up and take a ride with me?"

She wondered if she should be alone with him. Her heart acted so crazily when he was around and they struck so many sparks off each other, she knew it could be a volatile situation. His chuckle broke into her introspection.

"Do we need to list the pros and cons?" he asked.

She considered his knowing grin and had to smile. "A ride would be nice," she said demurely.

He watched as she saddled Sal, the mare she'd ridden previously, then gave her a boost up. When they were ready, he led the way down the ranch road. Honey noted his ease in the saddle and the way the stallion's hide gleamed a rich dark-red in the sun.

The world seemed new and wondrous this morning. The sages were right—confession was good for the soul. Her own felt lighter than it had in a long time. She didn't have to pretend anymore and watch every word she said.

Zack turned his mount to the left, then followed an overgrown path into the trees. The mare stayed close behind the stallion, so Honey didn't worry about guiding her. A short time later they came out on a flat rise.

"Whose house is this?" she asked, startled.

"Travis's." He rode past it.

She stopped in the yard. The mare dipped her head and munched on the dry grass. "Is this where he and his wife will live?" A thought came to her. "It was for his first wife, wasn't it?"

Zack swung down from the stallion's back. "Yes to both questions. I can see you're not going to be satisfied until you know all. Come on, I'll give you the ten-cent tour."

Zack opened the door and let Honey precede him into the house. Signs of recent work were all around. The house was almost finished. "It isn't a log house," she said. "The construction is modern."

"Very astute," Zack complimented. He visually examined the place. "It was to be Travis's gift to his wife. A new home for their new baby."

"How sad," she murmured.

The house was cozy, but big enough for a family. The kitchen was the center, with the living room opening into it. Four bedrooms and a laundry next to the garage, plus an office with built-in bookcases, completed the space.

"They must have been planning on a big family," she said, peering at the master bedroom.

"They wanted at least two or three kids," Zack said.

Honey entered the smallest bedroom, which was across the hall from the master bedroom, and imagined a nursery in there. Her best friend from high school had two children, and she'd often baby-sat and helped out with them when she'd lived in Los Angeles.

"Thinking about having some babies of your own?" Zack asked, his tone changing, becoming huskier and softer.

"Babies can be nice," she said. "I'm an honorary aunt to a three-year-old and a five-year-old." She laughed. "They can be a handful, but they can also be the sweetest things you've ever seen."

When she felt his chest brush her back as they stood in the doorway, she realized how close he had moved. Every nerve in her body sat up and took notice.

His hands on her shoulders gently urged her to turn to him. She did, her breath turning ragged.

"I've had trouble picturing you as the homebody type," he murmured. "Until now."

She shrugged slightly. "Home and family haven't figured very much in my life. I haven't had time to think about it."

With the lightest of touches, he rubbed his thumbs over her collarbones. "Are you thinking about it now?"

The question was sardonic, but all those possibilities for a future she'd never dared consider loomed before her.

Past experience reminded her of the danger in depending on anyone else for happiness. Present need coaxed her to say yes. "There are other things," she began.

"Yeah," he agreed. "But sometimes people have to find time for themselves and their own needs."

She shook her head. "I have to think of Adam. And your family's safety."

His eyes blazed, then he smiled.

She couldn't resist. Knowing a thing wasn't wise made no impression at all on the deep longing that rose up and engulfed her. Tilting her head, she gazed into those sea-blue depths and didn't care about complications or being wise or any of that.

"Sometimes," she whispered, "can't we simply have the here and now and not worry about anything else?"

"Yes." He bent and touched her forehead with his lips, then her temples, her nose, each cheek and finally her mouth in little skimming touches that drove her mad for more.

Stretching up on her toes, she locked her arms around his shoulders and let her body mold itself to his. Every plane and curve found its perfect place against him. The problem was that they felt so natural that way.

His chest lifted and fell when he released her mouth and pressed a flaming line of kisses along her neck. Finding the first button of her shirt, he opened it, then followed its line down her throat. The second. The third. Fourth. Fifth.

He pushed the material aside when they were all unfastened and cupped her breasts in his hands. He nibbled each tip through the satin of her bra, his touch teasing, his eyes tender as they engaged in the serious play of lovers. Behind her, he found the clasp and soon her bra was no barrier, either.

She wanted as much from him. Tugging his shirt free of his jeans, she quickly undid the buttons and opened it. He brought them together, flesh to flesh.

"It's like fire," she said fiercely.

"Yes. Everywhere we touch." He moved lightly against her, teasing her nipples by brushing against them in a gentle to-and-fro motion. "I love the feel of you. Sometimes I think I'm going to explode...when we sit at the table...or watch television...with others in the room."

He kissed her in a different spot on her face, neck or bosom with each pause.

"I want to catch you up in my arms and carry you to my room and make love to you for hours, then lie in bed and hold you…just hold you."

His words conjured up visions of delight. The hunger rose, swift and demanding. She caught his face between her hands and found his mouth. Their lips melded in a hot struggle for appeasement. It was impossible with only a kiss.

"This isn't enough," he whispered roughly. "I need all of you, everything you have to give."

For a second, for that brief instant of time when the world was new and anything seemed possible, she wanted to share all that she was with him and take all he could give.

But reality lurked behind every fantasy she'd ever known. So it was now.

When he raised his head and glanced around as if seeking a comfortable nest for them, she pushed slightly away.

"There's nothing here but the floor." He gave her a hopeful gaze.

She shook her head.

A rueful smile curved his lips. "I thought not," he admitted. "It's hard to let you go."

Letting silence speak for her, she eased back farther and refastened her clothing.

He frowned. "You're putting distance between us. Is that what you really want?"

"No, but there are too many complications." Finding the strength from deep within, she pulled away from his touch and the temptation of his embrace. "I don't want any entanglements. It's dangerous to be distracted."

His smile was so warm she nearly melted. "Far be it from me to suggest such a thing as dangerous as an entanglement. How about a nice old-fashioned affair?"

She returned the smile. "I don't think so."

Lifting a lock of hair, he studied it intently. "Your hair is growing out. Is the real you emerging, too?"

"I'm as real as I ever get," she told him on a lighter note. "I wonder if I should go all brunette. In case the men trace my whereabouts."

"No," he said in a low growl. "The dye seems to be disappearing. Let it." He caught her chin and held her face up so he could look into her eyes. "No more secrets, hear?"

She hesitated, then nodded.

A smile bloomed over his handsome features, causing her heart to turn over. It would be so easy and so foolish to love this man. She fought the temptation. The time would come when she had to leave, when she might have to flee to protect him and his family. "We should be going."

"Yeah, you're right. Caesar has had a sore leg. I need to see how he's doing, make sure he's not favoring it, before I put him back into training." He closed the buttons she'd opened in her eagerness to touch him.

They went outside and continued along the path,

which Zack explained was an old mining road from the 1890s. It was occasionally used for logging operations nowadays.

The ride lasted an hour, but the moment of tenderness was gone. Back at the ranch, they brushed down the horses and gave them each a bucket of oats.

"I'll be ready to go to town at eleven," Zack told her.

She nodded and hurried to her room to shower and change to slacks and a summer shirt. The temperature was in the seventies, the sky pure blue and the air like elixir. She wished she felt as buoyant.

"You coming back tonight for supper?" Uncle Nick asked as they headed out the door.

"Yes," she said, surprised at the question.

Uncle Nick looked at Zack for an answer.

He nodded. "I want to take Honey by Amelia's, though. I have an idea for a dance studio."

Intrigued now, she pressed him for an explanation when they got under way to Lost Valley.

"Amelia has a carriage house on her property. I think it has a large room with a wood floor. It could be used as a studio, but I don't know what shape the building is in."

Honey's mind reeled at the idea, that he would think of it, that this dream might become reality. Falling silent, she lapsed into a daydream about what could be, then laughed at herself for even thinking about it.

In town she rushed into the general store that served the community with groceries, medicines and miscellaneous items. She needed deodorant, shampoo, powder and other personal toiletries. Zack also had some shopping to do.

They met at the truck and headed for the B and B, which was on a side street at the edge of town. The house was a lovely old Victorian that had obviously been restored to its original glory.

Walking to the huge porch, she spotted Zack's car in a driveway winding toward the back of the building. He had a room here. The lovely redhead was his landlady. Honey refused to acknowledge the tiny spurt of jealousy that ran through her. Whatever she and Zack shared was fleeting. She would stay in the area only as long as it was safe for him and his family.

"Amelia," Zack called when they entered a large entry hall and sitting area.

A stone fireplace was the focal point of the room. Cinnamon and baking apples spiced the air. Honey realized she was hungry.

"In here." Amelia emerged from a linen closet and closed the door behind her. "Well, hello. Uh, Honey, isn't it? We met at the dance."

"You have a good memory," Honey murmured. "Yes, I'm Honey. I'm glad to see you again."

"We have a proposition to discuss with you," Zack told Amelia. "Do you have a moment?"

Amelia's eyes darted from one to the other before she nodded. "Let's go to my room. This way."

She led the way to a private sitting room overlooking an arbor and rose garden at the rear of the house. After serving tea, she sat down and looked at Zack.

"You have a carriage house behind the garage," he started. At her nod, he continued, "We were wondering if it was in good enough shape to use as a dance studio. Honey is thinking of starting her own ballet school."

She wasn't thinking any such thing, but she went along with the idea. "Not just ballet, but tap and modern dancing, too. Perhaps ballroom dancing for seniors."

Amelia's eyes lit up. "Why, that's a great idea."

"Yeah, but are there enough clients to support it, do you think?" Zack asked.

"If you offer a really wide variety of classes, I think there might be. The county has grown rapidly over the past ten years. Families are relocating up this way and commuting by car or by computer to their offices. It would certainly be worth the effort, but it might take a few years to establish a paying business. It took me three years to break even on *this* place. Advertising is the key."

"I've thought about both advertising and types of classes," Honey told the other woman. "Short, one-week or even one-day courses often work in a summer-vacation sort of environment. I'd like to make the classes fun for couples, something they can do together during a time of rest and relaxation."

"Dancing is relaxing?" Zack said.

Amelia and Honey laughed at his disbelieving tone.

"It is if you're good at it," Amelia said in defense of the idea.

"Ha," was his response.

"Some men enjoy dancing," his landlady informed him.

"Some men probably enjoy having needles driven under their fingernails, but I'm not one of them."

Honey envied the other two their easy repartee. After thinking at one time she was in love with the primo male dancer, she found out that he fell in love with all his lead female dancers. She'd avoided close associations within the dance troupe after that, even among the women.

Because of Adam, that had been the best policy, but sometimes she'd felt lonely, as she did now, listening to these two longtime friends chat. If she'd grown up here, if she'd known Zack all her life, if—

"Let's look it over." Zack suggested, bringing her back to the present. "You game for that?"

Honey nodded and he gave her a curious perusal. He'd known her mind was elsewhere. She'd kept her own counsel for so long it was difficult to share her thoughts or feel part of others' plans.

"You two go on," Amelia said. "If you think you can make it work, come back and we'll talk about what needs to be done. My assistant is off today and I have to stay close to the phone and front desk."

Zack propelled Honey out the back door and down a stepping-stone path. The driveway swept around a new garage and circled in front of the elegant old carriage house, then rejoined the driveway. Honey's heart thudded heavily as they went inside.

"Well?" Zack said after several minutes of silence. "Will it do?"

"The floor is good," she said. "With a sanding and a coat of varnish, it would be fine."

"The walls and ceiling need insulation and drywall. We could do that."

Honey cast him a doubtful glance. "We?"

"Sure. You. Me. The twins. The cousins. You would have to pay for the materials, but the work is no problem. Six baseboard heaters would handle the classes in winter. Come on. We can make a deal with Amelia about the rent. It should be pretty cheap since we'll do the fixing up."

"Wait!" Honey held up a hand. "We can't just rush out and jump right in. I have to think about a business plan and finances, a place to live, a license…"

"Seth will know what to do," he said with undaunted confidence. "He knows all that stuff."

She tried to think of other excuses.

"Look, will the place work or not?" he demanded.

"Well, it could. I mean, it has a lot of possibility, but—"

"Okay then, it's settled."

She pulled free when he tried to usher her out. "It's not settled," she told him sternly. "I'm not going to be railroaded into a rush decision."

"God forbid that you should be railroaded into anything," he practically snarled at her. "You should think everything out to the nth degree so you can be sure you're getting the best deal." He stomped out the door, then turned, holding it open for her. "Remind me to write you a check for the money I owe you."

She went outside. The sun shone warmly, so why did the day seem gloomier than it had ten minutes ago? "You don't owe me anything," she said in a subdued tone. "I came for my own reasons. I knew I couldn't possibly be Tink."

"The point is, you came. I said I would pay you." He headed toward the house, his jaw set in a stubborn line.

"If I stayed until the end of the month."

He stopped dead center on the path so that she nearly ran into his back. "Are you reneging on that?" he asked, rounding on her.

"I'm thinking of taking a room here in town. So I would be on hand to run the dance classes. It's too far to the ranch. Besides, I don't have a car."

He looked into her eyes as if searching for the elusive needle in a haystack, his eyes dark and turbulent. They stared at each other, then he muttered, "Damn," and reached for her.

Excitement wafted through her as his urgent but gentle—always gentle!—hands brushed over her arms and settled on her shoulders. Like the sunrise, light and warmth suffused her soul and she knew she could stay there forever.

"We should go," she said, pulling away and stepping quickly around him.

She could run from him, but she couldn't run from her heart. Despair and foolish elation jostled for position inside her.

Chapter Ten

When Honey and Zack returned to the house, Amelia had lunch prepared. "Stay," she invited. "We'll talk while we eat."

Zack declined and disappeared around a corner. Honey heard a door open and close somewhere down the long hallway.

"His room is there," Amelia explained, curiosity in her eyes. She didn't voice it. "Please have a seat. I'm eager to hear what you think."

For the next two hours, the women planned and plotted. They struck a tentative deal for the studio and for a room for Honey in the B and B.

"I have to talk to my brother," Honey said, leaving it at that, although Amelia gave her a questioning glance. She had to know if Adam thought it was okay to be in town or if it would endanger the friendly B and B owner.

Amelia insisted on showing Honey a room.

The bedroom wasn't large, but it had a view of the garden and part of the carriage house. The daybed was plush with pillows. A desk stood in one corner. That would be convenient for her laptop. The room had a sink, a closet and a chest of drawers. Two chintz-covered chairs and a small round table completed the furnishings. A full bathroom was next door.

"Actually you'll be doing me a favor by staying here. It isn't large enough for couples and few singles stop by."

"This is lovely," Honey said sincerely, pleased with the room.

It wasn't the luxurious space she had at the ranch, but for her, it was much more practical, being in town and right next to the carriage house where she would work. If that panned out. Swallowing hard, she sternly admonished herself not to let false hopes take root. However, she couldn't tamp down the little bubbles of excitement inside her.

"Zack's room is across the hall. I'll give you a key to the side door so you can come and go as you wish, too."

"Thanks," Honey said weakly, her heart bolting like a runaway pony.

With her savings and the deal Amelia had given her, she figured she could make it for maybe two and a half years without income. Provided she didn't buy any clothes or get sick.

Zack came out of his room and leaned against the door frame. "Satisfied?" he asked.

She nodded.

"Ready to head back?"

Again she nodded.

"What's wrong?" he asked quietly, sensing her doubts as always.

"I'm afraid."

He nodded as if he understood. "So am I."

"For your family?" she asked anxiously.

"For us."

His tone was portentous, sending fear crawling along her nerves. She knew he meant more than the immediate danger. "I don't want to hurt you. Or your family," she quickly added.

"Sometimes fate has other ideas." He gave her a ghost of a smile and a glance she couldn't read, then led her to the side driveway where his car was parked.

On the drive to the ranch, she sighed quietly as she watched the scenery go by. She knew the roads now. The trip wasn't nearly as daunting as that first time she'd come through here.

"Still feeling railroaded into a deal you don't want?" he asked.

"No, but starting one's own business is scary. I don't know if I can hold out for three years the way Amelia did."

"You can try it in Boise if this doesn't work out."

"Spoken like one who has never failed at anything," she murmured. She didn't mention the need to talk to Adam.

He stopped in front of the ranch house, shut off the engine and faced her. "We'll call Seth."

"Seth, the wise. He must be a prophet."

"Nah. He just knows everything."

She smiled and Zack chuckled. Inside, he went to the telephone and dialed his cousin. To her surprise, Seth came on the line at once. Zack explained the business proposition and motioned for Honey to get on the kitchen extension. She said hello when introduced and listened to Seth mull over the possibilities.

"Lost Valley has a population of a thousand," he said. "The area around it has another thousand. So that's two thousand. In the summer, the number swells to perhaps twice that, more on weekends, due to the outdoor activities. If you held regular weekend dances with a cover charge, you could probably bring in enough to pay your overhead and perhaps keep the school going during the winter months with smaller classes."

"Oh, I never thought of having dances. Doesn't the town already do that?"

"Only for special fund-raisers," Zack told her, "and not very often."

Seth knew the cost of a business license and advised her on the insurance she would need. He knew the law about serving alcohol, which she hadn't thought of.

"Amelia might go in with you on refreshments,"

Zack added. "Her guests could attend at a reduced rate. This could be good advertising for her—spend a week in the mountains and improve your dancing skills."

"Would that work?" Honey asked. "I'm not sure men would consider dance lessons a vacation."

"Yes, they would," Seth told her. "You just have to put it to them right, um, something to appease the little lady at night while the men get to fish all day."

Honey smiled wryly while the cousins laughed and agreed this was a great idea. After they hung up, Uncle Nick came out of his room and demanded to know what was so funny.

Zack explained.

"Hmm, if Seth thinks it would work, it most likely will," the older man said with the confidence she was beginning to associate with the Dalton gang.

When the twins came in, they had to be told the plans. Trevor volunteered both of them. "We can work on Saturday."

"Sorry, I'll be in Boise," Travis said. "Alison and I are attending a fund-raiser for her father. He's running for governor," he explained to Honey.

Trevor revised his plans. "I know some guys who will help. All we need are pizza and beer, and they'll show up."

"I can help later on, after the carpet is in," Travis promised.

"We'll get your house finished on time for the wedding, bro,'' Zack promised. He turned to Honey. ''Travis and Alison are getting married next month.''

Honey noted the quiet happiness in the engaged twin's eyes. ''That's wonderful,'' she said sincerely.

The men finished working out schedules and making plans. They thought everything would work fine.

''I really need to talk to Adam,'' she said. ''I can't do anything that might have an impact on his case.'' She looked at Zack. ''If the thugs show up, won't my presence endanger Amelia and the people in town?''

''No,'' he assured her. ''I'll be close.''

He exchanged a glance with her that sent her pulse racing as she recalled just how close they could be.

''This sounds complicated,'' she protested. ''I don't want to bring others into my problem.''

Uncle Nick laid a hand on her arm. ''You don't have to take on these men by yourself. I'm surprised your brother has left you alone to face this. I might have something to say to him when he shows up.'' Uncle Nick scowled fiercely.

Honey pitied her brother if Uncle Nick ever did confront him.

''We won't let anyone hurt you,'' Zack promised. ''My room is right across from yours at the B and B. Just yell when you need me.''

Honey felt the tide of blood sweep right up to her hairline as Uncle Nick and the twins looked from Zack to her. ''Men,'' she said. ''You think you're invincible.''

''Aren't we?'' Zack teased, his eyes alight.

"Leave her alone," Uncle Nick ordered, and turned to her. "You've carried a burden most men couldn't handle, but you won't be alone from now on. You have the Daltons on your side."

"And on your case if you don't cooperate with us," Zack tacked on.

Honey looked into four pairs of blue eyes and nodded. She knew when she was outnumbered.

By Tuesday night Zack was gritting his teeth to keep from shaking Honey. She wouldn't let him get started on the dance studio until she'd talked to her brother. According to her, she'd sent two e-mails to the man. She was in her room now, checking for answers.

Hearing her almost silent footsteps in the hall, he looked up expectantly from the ranching magazine he was pretending to read. She shook her head when she entered the living room and met his gaze. She was wearing the jacket he'd given her, he noted. That pleased him. At least she was willing to take that much from him.

"Going for a walk?" he asked, getting to his feet.

"Yes."

"I'll join you." He grabbed a fleece vest from the rack and slipped into it, then held the door for her. "Which way?"

"It doesn't matter."

He knew she liked the creek path and led her there. "The creek's down," he commented, feeling her silence like a brick wall. "The water won't last another month. That means the snowpack isn't very deep. We face serious drought by autumn when we don't get rain in the summer storms."

"I see," she said vaguely, making it obvious the words had no impact on her.

"Drought is a big problem," he continued, mostly to test her attention. "What are you worried about?"

Her eyes seemed as transparent as glass when she stopped by a log and stared up at him. "I have a rock in my shoe," was her answer. She sat down and removed the sneaker.

"Is it your brother?" he persisted, determined not to be left out.

She shook her shoe and brushed her sock, her head down now. He saw her silent sigh as she nodded.

"I haven't heard from him in ages. I worry that the men might have found him."

Zack sat on the log beside her. Her voice had dropped so low he could hardly hear the words. "Who would the police contact if he was injured?" he asked.

"They have my aunt's address and phone number."

"Have you checked with her?"

"I send her e-mails fairly often, so she knows how to contact me."

When she looked at him, her eyes so full of misery his insides squeezed into knots, he couldn't stand it. Looping an arm around her shoulders, he held her close while he sought words to ease her pain.

He felt miserable himself. Outside of family, he'd never been so acutely aware of another person's pain.

"I can check with the LAPD," he told her. "Do you know any of the detectives there?"

Her face filled with horror. "You mustn't! You could get Adam killed!"

She clasped her hands tightly together, a thing she did when stressed. "Easy," he murmured.

"Adam says we're not to trust anyone until he knows for sure what officers are involved in the drug deal."

Zack experienced the anger all lawmen feel when their fellow officers turn traitor. To protect and serve is a solemn oath. To violate that oath is the lowest form of betrayal.

"Okay, forget that. We'll just have to wait until we hear from him."

"What…what if we never do?"

"We'll face that when the time comes," he said, his own solemn oath to stand by her.

He realized he was in for the duration with this woman who had crossed his path—he paused to count—eighteen days ago. Less than three weeks, but it felt longer, as if he'd known her intimately almost from the moment they met.

Uncle Nick had once told him it could be that way, that bonds could form quickly, as if they'd been lovers in a past life.

Zack sighed and rested his cheek on her head when

she relaxed against him. "We'll get through this," he vowed. "It will be okay."

"Will it?" she asked, her soft voice etched with despair. "I'm tired of being afraid…"

As her voice trailed off, he knew she wasn't afraid for herself but for others—for her brother, for Uncle Nick and the family, for the people of the town. She touched him in so many ways he stopped trying to count them.

She stood suddenly. "When will it be over? This waiting and watching and not knowing anything—" Stopping abruptly, she took a breath and regained control. She even managed a faint smile. "It's the waiting that's brutal, isn't it?"

At the philosophical note, he could have kissed her. She was brave, this woman. His woman.

His woman?

Nah, he'd gone down the garden path last year and ended in the briar patch. He thought of Travis. After his wife and baby died, he'd gone into the hills and hadn't returned for more than a month. When he'd reappeared at the ranch house, he was lean and haggard. Zack remembered his brother's eyes. It was as if no one lived behind them.

As someone had once said, love could be hell. It sure as heck wasn't for him.

Honey steadfastly refused to start on the carriage house until she knew if she could stay in Lost Valley. Zack and Uncle Nick were definitely irked with her.

To them, once they'd decided on a course and Seth had declared it feasible, it was a done deal.

On another trip to town on Wednesday afternoon, she did consent to arrangements to rent a big sander from the local farm-and-home store.

"We'll get to work next week," she told Zack once they were back in his car.

"I have to work tomorrow, Friday, Saturday and Sunday," he reminded her.

"Fine. Monday is a good starting day. I'll surely have heard from Adam by then. I sent him an ad, which means he has to e-mail or call me as soon as he can. Unless…"

She couldn't voice the thought.

"Unless he's dead," Zack finished for her grimly. "Or he may have gone deep undercover, so that he can't risk even using a computer. That's a possibility."

"Yes." When Zack pulled into the parking lot at the sheriff's office, she shot him a questioning look.

"I've got to pick up a cruiser for tomorrow. I'll be patrolling some back roads for poachers. You can use the car to drive back to the ranch."

"I'd rather not." She felt shy about driving his car. It seemed to imply more than…well, more than friendship. She wasn't ready to go that far.

"Okay, leave it at the B and B. I'll pick you up before I head back to the ranch."

"Zack—"

He leaned over and kissed her on the mouth, a kiss

of controlled passion and patience. His tongue stroked her lips, then dipped inside when she opened them.

She was surprised and flustered by the public display, and more than shaken by his ardent attention.

"Don't," she managed to gasp when they ended the kiss. "It could put you in danger if someone thought you were involved with me."

His smile was maddening, part I-can-handle-anything male arrogance and part tenderness and passion and all the other unspoken things between them.

He chuckled. "Lady, we are involved, right up to your pretty little neck. Besides, I like kissing you." He shoved open the door and got out, leaving the engine running. With his long, sure stride, he disappeared into the nondescript brick building.

Honey slid over into the driver's seat and clipped the seat belt into place. Before she drove off, she noticed a man standing in front of the all-purpose store. He was looking her way. A shiver ran over her.

There was something vaguely sinister about him, something threatening in the motionless pose of his tall, muscular body. He wore camping pants of the type that could be turned into shorts by removing the legs, and a long-sleeved sage-colored shirt. His hat and beard disguised his features.

Abruptly she locked the doors and put the car into gear. All the way down Main Street and out to Amelia's place, she kept a careful eye on the rearview mirror, watching the road behind her more than ahead of her.

Before parking, she circled around the drive and stopped on the far side of the garage so she could see the street without being noticed easily. She sat there a long time before shutting off the engine and venturing out.

Keeping to the shade, she walked along the lawn edge and paused under the shadow of a willow tree, then observed the street in both directions. A pickup turned the corner, going very slowly—as if the driver might be looking for an address. Or following someone.

Her heart panicked, its beats jerky and fast, until she saw an elderly man driving, his white-haired wife in the passenger seat and pointing to a house farther down.

She managed a calming breath. No one else was visible for the length of the street. She didn't know if that was the norm for a weekday afternoon.

Feeling uneasy, she went inside and paid Amelia for the use of the small bedroom for a month. Having a place to call her own, separate from the Daltons, gave her a sense of relief and independence. She had a bolt-hole where she could hide and they wouldn't be involved if danger appeared.

Sighing, she sat on the bed, her mind blank, as if she'd thought all she could on the situation and her brain had nothing new to add. One thing, though, she wouldn't return with Zack to the ranch. There was no reason to.

A picture of the stranger appeared on her mental

screen. She shivered again. There had been danger all around him as he observed Zack and her.

"Dear God," she whispered, her heart raw with fear for the people of this peaceful valley. She shouldn't have come here. For her, there was no haven.

Chapter Eleven

"You have to go to the ranch," Zack told her at six. He stuck his hands on his hips and leaned against the door frame of her little room.

"I thought I'd stay here," she said, equally stubbornly.

"Think again. Uncle Nick is expecting us for dinner." He paused. "We can spend the night here. You'll need your pajamas and stuff, won't you?"

"I bought a toothbrush and a couple of things today. I thought I'd get all my luggage when you or someone had a moment to bring it to town."

His eyes narrowed. "So you'll just walk out. That's gratitude for you, after I brought you here and all."

"I don't owe you a thing. It was your idea that I was your long-lost cousin. I told you I wasn't."

He caught her hand and brought it to his lips. "I'm relieved about that."

The words died in her throat as she gazed into his eyes. "Passion makes people do foolish things. It distracts a person."

"You distract me," he said huskily.

When he would have pulled her into his arms, she dodged aside and paced across the room. "All right, I'll go with you, but just for dinner, then I want to come back to town."

"Okay."

The uneasy feeling pursued her as they made the drive out to the Seven Devils Ranch. The lights of the ranch house were a welcoming sight.

"The lights of home," Zack murmured as if reading her mind. "I always feel as if I've arrived at a safe harbor when I come here."

"Do you stay out here much?"

"On all my days off, so I can work with the horses. Otherwise the twins take care of them for me."

He parked the SUV, and they got out. Zack led the way to the door, then held it open for her. "Mmm, smells great," he remarked as they went inside.

"About time," Uncle Nick greeted them gruffly. He spoiled it by grinning and, to her surprise, giving her an affectionate thump on the shoulder. "Let's eat before dinner's ruined."

Honey hid a smile from the old rancher, who sounded like a distressed housewife fussing over supper. She and Zack washed up, then joined his uncle and brothers in the dining room.

"Zack says you've taken a room with Amelia," Trevor said, giving her a questioning glance while they passed platters of fried chicken and bowls of vegetables.

"Yes. It's a small room, but it'll do for my purposes. If I go ahead with the dance studio."

Zack told them about arranging for the sander.

"Good," Uncle Nick said to her. "I agree with the boys. You don't want to let it go too long, or we'll run out of time. Summer is almost over."

"I thought I might try classes for the next three months," she explained. "If it looks as if the classes will work and I'll have students for the winter, then I can invest money in insulation and inner walls."

Uncle Nick beamed at her. "I knew you had a good head on your shoulders."

"Thank you," she said, wondering if she was speaking the truth. By fall, she might be gone. Maybe by tomorrow.

Heaviness settled on her. Perhaps she was being paranoid, but she had a bad feeling about the stranger in town. Had he been sent to find her, to force her to contact Adam? Then would he kill them both?

"Don't look so glum," Zack said, his eyes sparkling with his usual good humor. "The best is yet to come. Shall I get the surprise?"

Uncle Nick nodded.

Honey realized something was going on. The men

looked too pleased with themselves as Zack disappeared into the kitchen. She heard a scratching sound and a couple of seconds later, smelled sulfur from a match.

He returned, carrying a cake with twenty-six candles on it. "Make a wish and blow out the candles," he ordered.

"It isn't my birthday," was all she could think of to say, as a confusion of emotions rushed through her.

"It's tomorrow, but I have to work, so Uncle Nick decided we should celebrate today. You did say the twenty-fifth was your birthday, didn't you? Did I remember right?"

"Yes, but I didn't expect anything."

"The cake is chocolate. Hope it's what you like. That's what all the kids always asked for," Uncle Nick said, obviously pleased with the surprise.

"My favorite," she assured him, touched by this gesture for her, a virtual stranger, one who had, furthermore, come less than honestly into their lives. There were gifts, too. She opened boxes and found chaps and a leather vest from Uncle Nick and the twins. Zack gave her a cowboy hat and a lariat of her own. Incredibly moved, she thanked them profusely.

While they ate the treat, the brothers told stories of past birthdays when they'd tried to give each other birthday whacks with one to grow on, which mostly ended up in a free-for-all. "Until Uncle Nick put a stop to it," Zack added wryly.

"Young hellions," their uncle said nostalgically.

"Including Roni. She was right in the middle of it all."

"Our girl cousin," Zack interpreted. "Veronica."

"Sounds as if you had a wonderful time." She tried not to feel envious of their childhood. Their parents had died, too, so it hadn't been all roses. Her gaze went to the smiling older man. They'd had Uncle Nick. She and Adam had had each other, so her life hadn't been all bad, either.

"Are you thinking of your brother?" Zack asked, leaning close to her ear while the twins discussed bringing cattle down from the mountain pasture early this year.

Her throat closed at his insight. She nodded.

"He sounds like a smart guy. He can take care of himself."

"Unless he's betrayed."

Zack frowned ominously. "Yeah, that's the one thing he can't guard against, a friend who goes wrong."

"Has that happened to you?"

His gaze focused on her. "No, but I'm not an undercover cop." He touched a finger under her chin. "Let's not borrow trouble. Your brother's been doing this for a long time. He'll be on his guard."

For some reason an image of the stranger came to her, causing a chill down her back. The fear was so real, so strong that she shivered.

"It's getting late," she murmured.

"And we have a long drive back to town. We're going to hit the road," he said to the others.

"Now that I have a room, I can take my luggage. You can have your guest room back." She smiled brightly.

"That's your room," Uncle Nick stated firmly, as if he'd never allow another in it.

She didn't argue. "You've all been so kind I can't begin to thank you."

"Keep us informed about your brother." Uncle Nick patted her on the shoulder before she left the room.

When she and Zack drove off, her three cases safely stowed in the rear of the SUV, she looked back once. The rambling log-stone-and-stucco house receded from sight. She felt as if she'd been tossed out of Eden. "You have a wonderful family."

"I agree. I wouldn't trade them for anyone else. Not even Trev," he added with a laugh.

She laughed, too. "Trevor is sweet."

"Ha." He gave her a sexy glance as he stopped at the county road, then pulled out. "I'm sweet, too. I'm hurt that you haven't noticed."

"You, sir, are arrogant."

His eyes narrowed in the dim light from the dashboard. "You'll pay for that insult, my lady."

His husky threat reached down inside her to a secret place that was vulnerable and needy. She wanted him and his strength and ardor, his incredible tenderness. Would it be terribly selfish to take tonight?

The question lingered in her mind all the way to town. They went in the side door of the Victorian. He made sure the dead bolt was secured before carrying her two larger cases to her door.

In the lounge, she heard a clock strike. "Eleven," she said, counting each bong.

"Yes." He dropped the bags by her door, then pushed his hat off his forehead and observed her with that smoldering look guaranteed to drive the unwary heart insane.

"Honey...?" he said.

His voice trailed off as if he wasn't sure what he wanted to ask, or if he should. She looked up at him and shook her head, denying the hunger between them.

"I'll be right across the hall if you need me," he promised huskily. "Just give me a yell."

"I will. Zack, thank you for...for everything. I'm glad I came home with you," she said impulsively.

"I don't want gratitude," he murmured.

He bent forward, his eyes on hers until his mouth touched hers. He closed his eyes and kissed her deeply. The passion flamed.

Long, breathless moments later, she unlocked her door and slipped inside without turning on the light. Zack gave her cases a shove inside with his foot, then closed the door behind him before reaching for her again.

They embraced as if this was their last night on earth, as if they were embarking on a perilous journey from which they might never return. The kiss was filled with mutual yearning.

She loved the feel of his body, strong and hard with masculine need. This, she thought, was where she belonged.

Oh, yes, yes, yes!

''Excuse me,'' a deep voice said out of the darkness.

Chapter Twelve

Honey stopped breathing. She knew that voice. "Adam?" she said. "Adam?"

The lamp flicked on. The stranger from town leaned against the wall next to the daybed, his eyes going from her to Zack, questions in the gray-blue depths.

"I take it this is the long-lost brother," Zack said wryly, releasing her from his embrace.

She realized he had shielded her with his own body when Adam spoke. "Yes," she said. "Adam, this is Zack Dalton, the deputy I e-mailed you about."

The men nodded to each other. The scene seemed surreal to Honey, like a dream she couldn't escape.

"How're you doing, pug?" Adam asked, turning to her and using the nickname he'd given her long ago.

To her chagrin, the tears came. She put her hands over her face. Zack clamped an arm around her and led her to a chair. He gently pushed her into it and grabbed a tissue from a box on the night table.

"I'm all right." She dried her eyes and blew her nose, then glared at her brother. "You were the man I saw earlier today, the one standing on the sidewalk and staring at me. I thought you were one of the enforcers. I thought they'd found me."

Adam looked grim. "They're hot on your trail. They traced an inquiry from L.A. to Vegas to here. Was that your cop friend here?"

She nodded. "It isn't Zack's fault. He didn't know what I was hiding from, but he knew something was going on. He called in a favor from a Vegas detective who traced me to L.A. and our aunt. He knew I'd lied about my name."

"What else does he know?" Adam gave Zack an assessing once-over.

"Everything. Zack and his family—"

Adam muttered an expletive.

Zack spoke up. "You don't have to worry about my family. They're solid. What are you doing here?"

Honey watched the men exchange glances. Zack inhaled sharply. "The enforcers are here," he concluded.

"Well, they're on their way."

"What's the plan?" Zack asked, making it clear he was counting himself in.

"I have some things I need to do first thing in the

morning, then we'll discuss it. I'm here for the trout fishing, by the way.''

She listened while the men talked, worry eating at her. In a few minutes they had agreed on a time and place to meet the next day. Then they both looked at her.

"Can you put me up for the night?" Adam asked.

"Of course." Heat rose to her face. If not for her brother, she and Zack would be in bed together at this moment. All three were aware of that.

Zack dropped to his haunches in front of her. "Do you want to stay with me?" he asked softly.

While the passion was there, so was the fierce need to protect. She shook her head. "I'd like to talk to Adam."

He nodded in understanding. "I'll see you tomorrow." With a nod to her brother, he left them alone.

"Are you in love with this guy?" Adam asked as soon as the door closed.

"Love implies commitment. I don't want to need anyone that much," she said dismally.

"Don't be afraid to grab hold of life," Adam said, studying her averted face, his advice surprising her.

"*You* haven't committed yourself to anyone."

"Do as I say, not as I do," he ordered on a gruff note. He yawned. "I'm dead—"

"Don't say that!"

"Sorry." His grin was unrepentant. "Can I sleep here tonight? I've rented a camper at a campground for tomorrow night, but it's not set up yet."

"Sure. Take the bed. Extra quilts are in the closet. I can make a pallet on the floor."

He arched a brow at her, reminding her of another arrogant male. "No way, pug. I'll take the floor. I'll be out of here before anyone stirs in the morning."

She pulled quilts, blankets and a pillow from the top shelf in the closet. Adam made a bed on the carpet under the side windows. "I'm sorry about all this," he said softly after they were ready for bed.

"It isn't your fault. It's just the way life is." She summoned a smile, then brushed her teeth and stored her case under the sink.

She couldn't burden Adam, who had enough to worry about, but she, too, regretted coming to Lost Valley.

With the lamp off, Zack stood by the window of his darkened room shortly before dawn, listening intently. He heard the soft snick of a latch as the side door was opened and closed. Cool air seeped into his room through the cracks around the door.

Standing to the side of the sash, he eased the shade open a slit and watched a dark figure move swiftly among the shadows of the trees and disappear down the street on foot.

Neither he nor her brother had slept much last night. A grim fury enveloped him as he thought of the men after Honey. No wonder she'd been frightened when they'd met at the casino.

He waited another hour so as not to disturb the rest

of the house, then went to the bathroom he shared with
Honey and showered, shaved and dressed in his uni-
form. Back in his bedroom, he left the door open to
the hallway until Honey appeared. "I'll swing by and
pick you up at eleven. I'm on duty today, noon until
ten," he reminded her.

She nodded, signs of fatigue in the shadows under
her eyes. He missed the old Honey—the shapely waitress, the fresh-faced youngster, the tenderhearted
woman who looked after the orphans at the ranch. She
continued to the bathroom and closed the door.

After buckling on the holster, he checked his gun
and ammo, then departed. In a few minutes he pulled
into the parking lot at the office.

The sheriff was waiting for him. "Zack, can I see
you in my office?"

"Sure." Zack glanced at another deputy, who
shrugged to indicate he didn't know what was up, then
grabbed a cup of coffee and joined his boss.

"Shut the door," the sheriff requested.

He did, then took the chair in front of the desk.
"What's happening?"

The sheriff, a distant cousin who'd been kin to the
original Dalton's wife, stared at him for a moment,
then spoke. "The FBI called this morning."

Every nerve in Zack's body went on double alert.

"Your assistance has been requested on a case they
hope to wrap up this week." The sheriff smiled wryly.
"An agent will contact you when he gets to town. It
has to do with money laundering and drugs." He shuf-

fled a folder on the desk. "I don't know how all this arrived on our doorstep, but there it is. That's the information I was given."

Zack decided there was no need for him to go into details about Honey and his earlier conviction that she was his long-lost cousin or that he'd brought her to Lost Valley.

The sheriff continued, "Keep me informed, will you? You can use Donnelly as backup if you need him."

Jase Donnelly was a friend. He was also a good cop. "I'll run everything I find out through him. He can keep you posted on what's going down. If I'm working with an undercover agent, I suppose I'll be undercover, too."

The sheriff stood and extended a hand. "I know you'll do the department proud."

"I'll do my best," he promised.

Things were looking up, he mused when he left the sheriff's office and checked the day's assignments. He noted he'd been crossed off patrol and put on special assignment.

A week. The FBI wanted to wrap things up this week. The case was developing fast. His heart thumped with excitement when he went outside. The town hadn't had a murder case in twenty years, and that had been a drunken brawl down at the campground on the Fourth of July. Other than a few domestic-violence incidents and a little robbery and rustling, it was a quiet community.

At ten before eleven, he swung by the bed-and-breakfast. Honey was on the front porch, sitting in a rocker. She dashed to the street as soon as she saw him and jumped into the SUV.

"I like a woman who's eager," he murmured.

She gave him a scolding glance, then clutched her purse in her lap. Tense again, he noted, angered anew that she was in danger. He drove to the roadhouse on the lake, a sort of honky-tonk bar that drew in the tourist trade.

Outsiders thought they were living dangerously when they came here, but it was really a family-run operation with a veneer of the Wild West. The obligatory moose head hung over the oak bar. He escorted her through the swinging doors and into the dim interior.

Not another soul was there.

The hair stood up on the back of his neck as he cast a quick look around. The place was silent as a tomb.

"Hi, y'all, come on in. That table has the best view of the lake," a young woman called, entering the dining room from the kitchen.

"You're new," Zack said.

"Right. I started last week. Cara had to return to New York. Her mom is sick."

"That's too bad," Honey murmured sincerely.

"Yeah. The special is barbecued ribs with fries and coleslaw. I can vouch for it." She set water and menus on the table and headed back for the kitchen. "Yell when you're ready to order. I'm working on the salad bar.''

The silence was strained after the friendly waitress disappeared. Honey sighed while looking at the menu. Zack saw her glance take in the lake area, then go to the door several times.

A minute later the swinging doors opened and a man walked in. Zack recognized the tall, muscular form at once. Across the table, he heard Honey's sharp intake of breath.

He studied her brother over the top of the menu. Adam did a slow survey of the room, not seeming to notice them at first. Then he looked directly their way.

A smile tugged at Zack's mouth. If he hadn't known the man, he would have recognized him by the eyes. They were a replica of Honey's.

''Join us?'' he invited.

''Don't mind if I do,'' the brother said.

Honey breathed a sigh of relief. Zack acted as if he knew Adam, which fit in with her brother's plans.

After they had all ordered the special and iced tea, Adam leaned forward. ''FYI, I'm Adam First,'' he said.

''First?'' Honey inquired.

''As in, the first man,'' Zack told her.

''Right,'' Adam complimented the deputy. ''It's going to be a pleasure working with you.''

''What exactly are *we* going to be doing?''

''Watching out for Honey.''

She frowned at both men as they exchanged a smile and a glance at her, then resumed their conversation.

Adam filled Zack in on the drug operation, his blown cover and how Honey became involved. "I'm sorry about that, pug," he said. "She had to give up her career and go into hiding," he told Zack, his regret obvious.

"So she said."

"I'm thinking of opening my own dance studio," she mentioned in the silence that followed the arrival of the waitress, who served tall glasses of iced tea. "Amelia, who owns the B and B, said I could rent her carriage house. Of course we have to fix it up first."

"With all of us working, it'll be ready in no time," Zack assured her. "My family and I are going to help."

The waitress departed. Honey noted the interested perusal of the two men, then the envious glance tossed her way as the younger woman left them, and knew what she was thinking. A woman should be so lucky to have two handsome men take her to lunch. Honey considered it lucky that her brother was still alive. She sighed.

Adam studied her, then Zack. "You must have an honest face. Honey doesn't usually trust people at first sight."

"Well, she didn't think much of me right off the bat," Zack drawled. "But the Dalton charm prevailed."

Honey smiled while the men chuckled. Their meal arrived. Zack ate quickly after checking his watch.

"In a hurry?" Adam asked.

"I have duty today," Zack began, then stopped. "Special assignment," he added. "I guess I'm on duty now. You're the one who was to contact me?"

"Right."

"How do we watch out for her?" Zack asked, aware of the kisses the brother had witnessed. "A beginner could pick any lock at the B and B. The ranch is the safest place. My brothers live there." His eyes narrowed in thought. "We could use an extra hand… No, you're an old college friend who happened to drop by for a visit?"

"I took night courses in law enforcement in L.A.," Adam said. "Is that where you went?"

Zack shook his head. "College in Boise. Police academy in Denver."

"I was on a case in Denver for a year."

"Okay, that's where we met," Zack agreed.

"I worked for a construction company there," Adam continued, "and nearly froze when winter came."

Honey was silent as the men planned their mutual past down to the month and year of their friendship. Other people came into the restaurant as the noon hour got under way. The men switched to "reminiscing" about the good old days in Denver. Listening to them, she could almost believe they really were old friends.

"Remember that time we went hiking and got

lost?'' Adam said. ''We found some berries, but the local bear thought they belonged to him. He rose up on his hind legs—he was about twenty feet tall—and clacked his teeth at us.''

''Ah, he was little,'' Zack drawled. ''No more than twelve or fourteen feet at his shoulder.''

''What did you do?'' she asked, acting her part as the wide-eyed naif.

''Well, I figured I could outrun ol' Zack here, but he grabbed my shirt and said we had to stand up to the bear. He yelled and waved his arms, then threw rocks. I stood there with my mouth hanging open, sure we were going to be the main course, served rare and already stuffed with berries.''

''You city dudes,'' Zack said, and shook his head.

Honey laughed. So did the couple at the next table and the waitress, who was taking their order.

When the three of them finished and went outside, Adam became serious. ''Can you pretend to be on patrol or somehow account for cruising around?''

''Sure.''

''We're looking for two strangers. My sources say they may be posing as bikers, Hell's Angels without the tattoos.''

Zack stopped beside the cruiser. ''Are they looking for you or Honey?''

Adam shrugged. ''Either or both.''

''You're using her for bait.''

Zack's tone was harsh, almost challenging. Honey tensed as Adam gave the deputy a long appraisal.

"If we don't clean this bunch up, she'll be on the run the rest of her life. We already have the cop who squealed on me in custody. He's singing nicely—the whole opera. As soon as we pick up the enforcers, the L.A. vice squad will move in on the others," her brother said.

He smiled, and it was a dangerous thing. Her insides clenched as she considered the options.

"I want to get the two thugs who would harm an innocent woman," Adam added in a low tone. "Nothing is sacrosanct to them. They'll finish the job they were paid to do, no matter what happens back in L.A."

"Shouldn't I stay in town?" she asked. "That way, I'll be available for them to spot me sooner."

"You need to act normally," Adam told her. "Work on your dance-studio project. Visit the ranch. Pretend you're part of one big happy family."

"Okay," she said doubtfully. "I wish I could do more."

"Being the bait isn't enough?" Zack hooked a hand around her neck and pretended to squeeze. "You'll give me gray hair yet."

Adam glanced at them, then surveyed the area while he talked about fishing. Zack pointed out the best fishing holes around the lake as he answered questions about the area and tossed in some info on the amount of backup they could expect if they needed help.

Honey sensed a return of the earlier tension. If she hadn't agreed to accompany Zack, his home wouldn't now be threatened by gunmen. Sometimes she felt that she was nothing but trouble to everyone who knew her. Her aunt had told her that many times, usually after a fight with her cousin.

"I'm staying in an RV at the campground and have a pickup there," Adam said. "How about showing me the way to the ranch? I want to scout out the area between here and there with an eye toward an ambush."

He guided them to his rented RV. They waited while he backed out of his parking space and fell in behind them on the road leading out of town and to the ranch.

"You're quiet," Zack commented after a bit.

"Just thinking," she said. "Life is complicated and dangerous." She looked back at Adam.

"Everything will work out," Zack said with a return of his usual male confidence. "It isn't your fault."

She gave him a faint smile. "Right. I only brought danger and destruction to the valley, but no matter— right will prevail."

"I was the one who laid down a trail that brought the thugs directly to you."

"Great," she muttered. "Both of us can walk around in sackcloth and ashes, feeling guilty as sin."

He hesitated, then said softly, "You've won a place here, Honey. Uncle Nick, the twins, all of us have come to care for you. So don't feel guilty. We're glad to help a friend in trouble. Besides, I'm glad to have a beautiful woman in my debt.''

When she gazed at him, he flashed her a wicked grin. Her good intentions went up in smoke. She'd thought to distance herself from him and his family by living in town, but it wasn't going to be that simple, not with Adam and Zack working together on the case. She felt like a pawn trapped between two powerful kings who happened to be on the same side and aligned against her.

''Hey, look who's here,'' Zack said cheerfully when they arrived. ''More family.''

Adam parked beside the SUV, and they all went into the house together.

''About time,'' a female voice called out.

''Roni, ol' gal,'' Zack greeted the pretty, petite woman who came out of the kitchen, wiping her hands on a towel.

A man followed. ''Hey, Zack.''

''Well, heck, is Beau here?'' Zack demanded.

''Do I hear my name being taken in vain?'' another male voice called out. Beau appeared behind the other man.

Zack introduced Roni, her brother Beau, who was the doctor Honey had met previously, and the sixth cousin, Seth. The wise one, as Honey had named him to herself.

Seth was a startling contrast to the other five cousins. She knew he was the oldest. Instead of the Dalton blue eyes, his were almost black. His skin was darker, too, perhaps Latino or Native American. His hair was thick and straight, no sign of the stubborn wave over the forehead the other male cousins had.

Roni was a surprise, too. She had the blue eyes and the dark, wavy hair, but she was a Dresden-doll version of the family—small and delicate and beautiful.

"Roni, Seth, this is Honey." Then Zack gestured toward Adam. "And this is an old friend who's come up for the fishing and may help us out on the ranch this summer—Adam First."

So, he was going to keep up the pretense with his family. Honey was glad she'd left the introductions to Zack.

"Where's Uncle Nick?" he now asked.

"Out at the barn with the twins," Seth answered. "We might have a new colt or filly by now."

Roni tossed the dish towel over a chair. "Let's go see, shall we?" She gave Adam a bright smile, boldly took his arm and led the way outside.

Honey wasn't sure how she felt about this blatant possession of her brother. She and Zack followed the couple with the other cousins right behind.

Again Zack introduced Adam as an old friend to the rest of the family. Adam nodded to the twins and shook hands with the older man, who studied him for long seconds.

"Adam," Uncle Nick said in a thoughtful manner. "You're Honey's brother."

Zack laughed while the others looked questioning. "We may as well tell all," he told Adam.

Adam nodded and smiled at the petite brunette who stood beside him, her gaze filled with speculative intelligence.

"Honey's brother," Zack agreed with a wry glance at his uncle. "Okay, here's the plan. It's top secret, so lock it in your mental vault."

He told them what was happening in a few terse sentences. When he finished, the Daltons were furiously indignant that the gunmen were after a lone woman.

"You've come to the right place," Seth told her. "No one will be able to hurt you here."

Adam dropped an arm around her shoulder. "Well, pug," he said, "I asked for one Dalton to work with me on the case. I had no idea we were going to get a whole gang."

Honey noticed his gaze was on Roni as the group laughed. Roni returned the gaze.

Troubled, Honey wondered if she should warn Roni that her brother had always traveled fast and always—*always*—alone. He'd never fallen in love that she knew of.

But there was always a first time.

She sighed, not wanting either Zack's cousin or her brother to get hurt. The same went for Zack and herself.

The question was, were they truly interested or was the attraction just physical? She sighed again, not sure of anything.

"Let's go inside," Roni said, taking charge of the

group after they admired the new filly. This time she fell into step beside Honey. "Uncle Nick told me you had a birthday celebration yesterday without the rest of us. I'm miffed about that."

Honey didn't know what to say.

"So," Roni continued, "I demanded another one tonight. I baked the cake."

"Don't worry," Beau told them, "I brought my medicine kit with me. And a stomach pump."

He and Roni staged a mock fight. Seth pulled a quarter from his pocket and announced his money was on Roni. No one took up his bet.

Again Honey was assailed by regret. She'd brought the enemy into this charming paradise. It was her duty to see that the bad guys were apprehended as quickly as possible and life resumed its normal course for the Dalton family.

Adam would leave as soon as the case was wrapped up just as he always did. What would she do? She glanced at Zack and found his eyes on her.

Warmth speared through her. Did she dare think her wishes could come true this time? She smiled slightly as hope responded with a joyful leap that made her giddy.

Foolish heart, to have such dreams....

Chapter Thirteen

Zack was exasperated with Honey when they left the ranch and returned to town. Adam had left before them and presumably was at the RV campground. Roni and Seth had headed back to Boise after a hilarious dinner of teasing and storytelling. Beau was spending the night at the ranch.

Honey slanted Zack a glance as he pulled into the space beside the garage at the B and B. Yes, he was still angry. He'd wanted her to stay at the ranch. She'd refused. Neither Adam nor anyone else had been able to change her mind.

Just before they'd left the homestead, she thanked Uncle Nick for his hospitality and apologized for putting his family at risk. The older man had dismissed her gratitude. He'd told her she was brave and loyal and caring.

"Just the sort of person I would want my daughter to be," he'd added as they'd said their farewells.

His words had nearly made her cry in front of everyone.

"Here we are," Zack said in a near snarl as he removed the keys and climbed out of the SUV.

She preceded him to the side door, unlocked it and went inside. At her room, with the door open, she faced him. "I had a wonderful time with your family, Zack. So did Adam."

"Good," he said brusquely. "Make sure your door is locked with the dead bolt and that the chain is on."

"I will." She didn't go inside.

He paused after unlocking his own bedroom door. His eyes, a fathomless blue as endless as the sea, met hers, and she couldn't look away. He muttered a curse.

"I never know where I am with you," he growled, but the anger was gone.

Fire of a different nature seared her at his stare, then she was in his arms, his mouth hot and ravenous on hers. She clung to him, helpless to fight the desire that flowed between them.

"Wait," he said.

He removed the key from his lock, then simply picked her up in his arms and crossed the threshold into her room. With a booted foot, he pushed the door closed behind them. The latch clicked into place. Then he kissed her again.

His embrace answered all the wild cravings in her. He was everything she'd dreamed of finding in her rosy view of the world during her adolescence. She returned his kisses with a desperate yearning as their caresses deepened. When they were breathless, he released her lips and trailed moist kisses along her throat.

"Prince Charming," she murmured. "You consume me with your kisses, yet I want more."

He lifted his head. "I know. Kisses aren't enough."

His hands roamed her back, swept the curve of her hips and urged her tightly against him, then moved upward. He palmed her breasts as if testing their weight. His groan of need fed her own.

Unable to stop, she moved lightly against him until he caught her in a tight embrace. His heart thundered in accompaniment to hers. His eyes were dark now, his desperation as great as her own.

"I wish we had met long ago, before…before everything," she whispered raggedly.

Zack heard the sorrow and wished he could ease her worry. "It'll be okay," was all he could say to reassure her. "Adam and I will make sure of that."

She ran her fingers into his hair. "I don't want either of you hurt."

"Then stay," he said.

She stiffened against him. He wanted the sweet yielding of her body to his and held her more closely.

"Stay?" she repeated.

"Build a life here." When she moved away, he reluctantly let her go. "Okay, this isn't the time," he said, making light of the moment. "But think about it. We'll talk later, after things are resolved."

"People may be dead by then."

Her smile was infinitely sad, but there was no fear in her eyes, only concern and despair. His heart swelled with pride. She had courage.

"Not me," he said. "Not you. Nor Adam."

Her laughter was hollow. "Do you have a crystal ball?"

He laid his hands on her shoulders. "I have confidence that we'll all be on the alert. We'll watch each other's backs. You won't go anywhere without having me as a shadow."

When she searched his face, he held still and tried to let her see all the way to his soul, a thing he'd never done with anyone.

Feeling a tremor rush over her, he knew he could overcome her scruples and share a night of wild passion in her arms. The hunger gnawed at him. He stepped back. She had to come to him willingly.

He flicked the tip of her nose and witnessed the indecision in her gaze. "It's okay. There'll be other times for us. Save that thought."

Smiling, he left her, closing the door and waiting until he heard the dead bolt click into place before going into his room.

As he prepared for bed, he considered the future. He knew of a two-acre lot on the lake that was for sale. It had an old house that would need fixing up, but the place was great for her plans, close to town and the B and B and not so far that she couldn't visit the ranch and Uncle Nick on occasion.

Yeah, it would be perfect. Now all he had to do was convince her.

Amelia looked relieved when she spotted Honey the next morning. "Something has come up, and we need your help," she said when Honey and Zack were seated.

Honey was surprised. "What is it?"

"The music teacher fell down the steps to her basement yesterday. She's in the hospital in Boise with pins in her leg to hold the bones in place while they mend."

"Oh, that's terrible," Honey said in sympathy, but seeing no connection to herself.

"She was in charge of a musical to raise money for an amateur theater group we hope to start here."

Honey began to see where this was leading.

"We need someone to take over," Amelia concluded, smiling expectantly at her. "Would you do it?"

Honey shook her head. "I don't play the piano or anything."

"That's okay. We have someone for that. We need someone to direct and make up some dance routines."

"What kind of show is it?" Honey asked, interested in spite of herself.

"A musical featuring Broadway hits. You'd be perfect for it and an angel to help us out."

The show might be a good thing. After all, Honey had decided last night to make herself "visible" to the men looking for her.

If, by being in the open as much as possible, she could force them to make their move, the danger would soon be over for everyone, and life could get back in its groove. She and Zack could explore the attraction between them as a normal couple. Her heart raced as she thought of the future.

"Do it," Zack said, breaking into her thoughts.

"I think I should see what they're doing first," she told the other two. "If I can help, I will."

"Good. We meet tonight at seven at the community center, where the dance was held. I've got to call the others." Amelia dashed to her office as if it was a done deal.

"Well," Zack drawled as they went to the buffet, "this will put you in the limelight."

"That's what I was thinking." She gazed up at him, wondering if they were being wise.

He touched her shoulder lightly and withdrew. "Then it will be over."

She nodded and picked up her cup. "What shall we do today?" she asked brightly.

"Oh, we'll think of something."

He gave her a wicked grin that sent fire racing along her nerve endings. "Let's walk by the lake," she quickly suggested.

He agreed and then laughed as if he hadn't a care in the world. There was a daredevil air about him, as if he was ready and eager for action, an attitude she'd seen in her brother when he was onto something big.

"Sometimes I wonder about men," she muttered, reaching for an English muffin and a peanut-butter packet.

"I personally do a lot of wondering about women, one in particular."

She frowned at his come-hither glances, but was unable to quell his high spirits. He continued his sexy hectoring over the meal. Happiness rose within her, as buoyant as a life raft, and she couldn't hide the smile that spread across her face.

"Ah, at last," he said, touching the corner of her mouth, then bringing his finger to his lips as if stealing a kiss from her.

By ten that evening, Honey knew the musical numbers by heart. By eleven, she had a clear idea of the dance numbers she needed to choreograph.

"Thank you so much for taking over," the lead female performer said again. This was echoed by several others as they grabbed their jackets and prepared to head home.

Honey had been thanked so much it was getting embarrassing. "Actually it was fun," she said, realizing the evening had flown.

"Lights out in five minutes," Amelia called.

Amelia had a very good voice and could play the

guitar. In addition to her and the piano player, they had a drummer, a bass violinist and two more guitar players to provide backup for the musical review. If they managed to save enough money, they were going to buy curtains and stage props for the community center, then put on plays and other musicals during the summer months.

"How did it go?" Zack asked, coming forward from the back of the room.

"Fine. The group was much better than I'd expected. Amelia could perform professionally," she said, giving praise where it was due. "She sounds as if she has a trained voice, but she says she hasn't."

"I've heard her sing. I agree. She's very good."

Honey nodded as they went outside. Amelia, who had waited in the foyer for them, made sure the door was locked before she headed for her car. Honey and Zack were in his own car. He'd dropped off the cruiser at the sheriff's office while she'd followed in his car prior to their arrival at the community center.

He opened the passenger door and glanced inside before letting her in.

Amelia drove off, and they were the last ones in the parking lot. Honey looked around while Zack got in and started the engine. She wondered if Adam was hiding in the shadows, watching and waiting for the two enforcers to show themselves. An ambush would be easy from those trees next to the entrance.

A hand touched hers. "I can hear the wheels turning from here," Zack said in an amused voice.

"I was worrying about someone lurking in the trees," she admitted. Her heart lurched when she thought of Zack's getting hurt. He would defend her to the death. She knew that as surely as she knew the sun would rise in the east in the morning.

When they reached the B and B, she laid a hand on his arm. "Come inside," she invited.

"I intend to," he said.

In her room he made sure the blinds were drawn, then searched the room as if looking for something he'd lost.

"What are you doing?"

"Checking for any possible hiding places I might have missed and for any signs of a previous search."

"Do you see anything?"

He turned, his hat in his hand, his smile in place, his eyes...oh, his eyes!

"Only a beautiful woman," he said.

"Don't play games. This is serious."

He walked to the door and paused. "I've never been more serious in my life," he said softly.

She hesitated, but she'd known from the moment they'd arrived that she had lost the battle with her conscience. Taking two steps, she put herself between him and the hallway door. No words came to mind. She could only stare up at him as yearning overcame her common sense.

His eyes darkened. "Is this an invitation?"

She nodded.

"Thank God," he murmured reverently.

Then he took her into his arms. He was everything she remembered—tender and gentle and ardent, his big, careful hands taking possession of her body until she panted with longing.

''Come to me,'' she whispered, touching him as intimately as he did her. They made love on the narrow bed, in the padded chair, and when they woke shortly before dawn, perched on the chest in front of the window. They slept late.

Honey walked to practice on the Friday afternoon of the following week. She had to force her mind to serious matters after spending the past several nights in Zack's arms. She smiled as she recalled their cramped quarters in her twin-size bed the first night before moving to his room.

As she strolled along Main Street—she was being ''visible,'' as per Adam's plan—she was greeted by several people, one of them Danny, whose arm was still in a cast. He told her he was looking forward to attending the show and would toast her with champagne at the cast party afterward. The bass violin player waved from the grocery, where he was the manager.

Odd, this adventure with Zack had started a mere month ago, but in that short span of time, she'd made friends in the town, had fallen in love with the ranch and his uncle and become Zack's lover.

This was hasty behavior for her. Usually she had to know someone a long time to feel close to them.

Passing the grocery parking lot, she noticed two men there. They were putting groceries in a carrier on the back of a motorcycle. Another big bike was parked beside the first. One of the bikers glanced her way.

She clasped the strap of her purse as fear flashed through her. Keeping her gaze straight ahead, she walked on as if she hadn't a care in the world. In a minute she heard the bikes start up.

The two men passed her and headed out toward the campground. Turning her head slightly, she met the gaze of the bigger one of the two. He smiled and nodded.

She did the same. Her breath eased as she entered the lane that wound through the tiny city park to the building in the center. No one would be crazy enough to come to town looking like refugees from a motorcycle gang. It was too conspicuous.

Several people were at the civic center, including Zack, when she arrived. Dressed in snug jeans and a chambray shirt, he looked very much at ease as he helped unload folding chairs for the two performances, which were to be held tomorrow afternoon and evening. He smiled when he spotted her.

Her heart drummed against her breastbone while she pretended not to see him. She went inside, checked her watch and called the performers together. She had each group go to a different part of the building and rotated among them, giving them directions and tips until they got their parts down pat. Two hours later she called for everyone to be seated, then started the show from the beginning.

There were a few mix-ups, which brought laughter, but overall, it went well. Everyone applauded when it was over.

"Dress rehearsal tonight? Was that the plan?" she asked before the group broke up.

"Right," Amelia said. "I can't believe how smoothly it's going. It makes a difference having a professional take you through the routine." She smiled approvingly at Honey. "You want a lift to the B and B?"

"It's so beautiful I'd rather walk."

Honey waited until the others had left. Going outside, she noted that Zack and the other men had finished their chores and also left. The loneliness she'd experienced most of her life returned like a dropped rock.

The trees partially obscured her view of the main road through town. It was late afternoon now and the shadows were deep under the oak trees. A spot of brightness caught her eye, and she realized dandelions were in bloom, looking like sunlight scattered around the edge of the woods.

Slowing, she breathed deeply of the pure mountain air and gazed at the snowy peaks west of town. The ranch was tucked into its own little valley, a world unto itself, and she wished she could be there, safe and happy.

With Zack.

It came to her that she'd never felt this intensity, this passionate longing for another person before, not as an adult. Whatever happened, she would never regret this past week in his arms.

She made it through town without incident and arrived back at the lovely Victorian house. Zack's door was open when she went inside.

"You forgot to lock your room when you left," he told her, but there was no reprimand in his tone. Instead, his eyes were warm and welcoming.

She refrained from throwing herself into his arms. "Did you go in?"

He nodded. "No signs of entry," he said in a low voice.

"I saw two men at the grocery. They were on Harleys."

"Adam spotted them, too. They arrived yesterday and are staying at a cabin on the lake. They went fishing early this morning, then ate lunch at the restaurant on the lake."

"Are they…?"

"Maybe," he said casually, urging her into the room and closing the door. He kissed her deeply, then grinned. "I've been waiting for hours to do that."

She turned from him and gazed blindly out the window at the roses climbing up an arbor. "We have to stay alert."

He tipped her head to face him. "No harm will come to you," he promised.

"Or to you?" she asked.

His eyes delved into hers. "Are you worried about me?"

"Of course. You, Adam, anyone who's in the way when they make their move could get hurt. I wish we could arrest them now."

"They haven't done anything yet." He moved to the side window and checked the driveway and garage.

"Adam has drummed that into me for years. Even when he's positive a crime has been planned, without solid proof he has to wait until it's being executed before taking the perps down. It's difficult to wait, though."

"Tell me about it." Zack tossed her a rueful smile over his shoulder. "Professional gunmen usually move quickly once they spot the victim. I'm sure they know where you are."

She stood silently while he sat in an easy chair and flicked on the television to a Boise news channel.

The weather was to continue fair and sunny during the day, cool at night, the weatherman told them. The anchor said a state politician was involved in a sex scandal.

Zack snorted at that.

To her shock, a public announcement of the musical in Lost Valley was announced. The reporter urged everyone to turn out for the show after the music teacher explained what it was for. They showed an excerpt of Amelia playing her guitar and singing a lovely ballad. Honey realized the interview tape had been filmed before the teacher had fallen down the stairs.

"Too bad they didn't have you on," Zack said. "That would have gotten the enforcers' attention."

"Thanks."

He chuckled, then reached for her hand and gently tugged her onto his lap. "How shall we pass the rest of the afternoon?" he inquired, his smile as gentle as his touch, but his eyes…a woman could get lost in those eyes.

She rested her head against him and was content to listen to his heartbeat. They stayed that way until it was time to go out to eat. He went with her, acting very much the attentive lover.

"Aren't I supposed to be alone as much as possible?" she asked as they returned to the community center for the evening's dress rehearsal.

"No. You're involved in the community. You have a boyfriend. Everything looks normal."

She wondered for how long, but didn't voice the worry as she went inside and started the rehearsal. Soon she was caught up in the music and the performances.

Zack watched the show take shape under Honey's skillful direction. She moved the amateurs along with patience and humor and brought the musical to a close nearly on time. He couldn't stop a surge of pride when everyone gathered around Honey at the end. The place sounded like a happy beehive, he mused, and she was at its center.

Forcing aside personal thoughts, he checked that no one had entered the building when the volunteers left in groups of twos and threes, chatting the whole time and calling out to others. They were pleased with the show and their excitement hummed in the night air.

Amelia and Honey were the last two out. Amelia made sure the door was locked and went to her car. His heart quickened its cadence as he realized he and Honey were alone, illuminated in the silent parking lot by the four high spotlights at its corners.

Now, he thought, and instinctively pulled her close, sensing a change in the air, like an animal catching a scent on the wind.

She glanced up at him once as they walked to his car. Her smile was faint, but her eyes held no fear.

"I have a feeling—" He stopped as a sound like an angry wasp whizzed past them. "Down," he said, drawing his weapon from under his jacket.

Honey didn't wait. She dived for the ground beside the car and rolled into the shadows under it. Zack crouched on the gravel beside the passenger door. She saw he held a gun in his right hand. The whizzing sound by her head had been the passage of a bullet, she realized. The enforcers were using a silencer.

A flash in the woods caught her attention, then the funny buzz again and rock scattered near the front tire.

"Stay put," Zack ordered, and was off, bent low, running from shadow to shadow when he reached the lawn and the trees scattered about, following the bullet to its source.

Honey stared into the night, waiting for another flash from the gunmen, but nothing happened. She heard two muffled pops in the darkness. She remained as still as possible. The silence lengthened.

Lights appeared suddenly in the woods. "Okay," she heard Adam call, "we got 'em."

Quickly she scooted from her hiding place and ran toward the trees that lined the lane. She found Adam and another policeman with the men. The enforcers were now in handcuffs and lying on the ground. To her surprise, they weren't the two bikers.

"Where's Zack?" she asked.

The other cop glanced at her as he spoke into his radio. "Officer down. We have an officer down."

Honey's heart dropped to her shoes. "Where is he?"

"Here," Adam said, kneeling in the nearby shadows.

She rushed to the figure on the ground. The wound, high on Zack's left shoulder, was pumping blood. "He's wearing a vest. How could he be hurt?"

"The bullet came at him from an angle, going between the vest and his shoulder," Adam explained.

"I'm okay," he assured her, but the painful grimace that followed belied the words.

"Shut up," she said, and pressed her fingers over the hole.

"I love a bossy woman," Zack told her, then his eyes closed and he was unconscious.

The wail of several sirens rent the cool night air. In

a few minutes paramedics from the county fire department had administered to the wounded deputy. The sheriff and several of his men took charge of the gunmen and cordoned off the area with police tape.

Honey stood by, not sure what to do.

"Go with him," Adam said, giving her a push toward the medical truck. The medic didn't say a word when she climbed into the back and took Zack's hand.

"Can you tell how serious his wound is?" she asked.

"I think it missed the lung, so it probably isn't as serious as it looks."

"Where are you taking him?"

"The sheriff's office. A helicopter will airlift him to the hospital in Boise. It won't take long," he said, sympathy in his manner.

"He has a cousin who's a doctor. Beau Dalton. He lives in the city, I think."

The paramedic grinned. "I went to school with the Daltons. Beau has already been called. He told us to meet him at the hospital." They were silent the rest of the trip.

Honey stood alone on the tarmac after the helicopter took off, but the deputies in on the arrest arrived in a few minutes. The two gunmen, dressed in nondescript jeans and dark shirts, were locked up. Adam arrived with the keys to Zack's car. "I thought you might need transportation," he said, handing them to her.

"What was this all about?" one deputy asked another as they went inside.

"Those guys are hired guns. They were supposed to kill someone," the other answered.

"None of this would have happened," Honey said to Adam, "if I hadn't come here. No one would have been hurt."

"Don't go on a guilt trip. It was me they wanted. They knew I'd show up to protect you. My contact in the gang sold me out. He set us both up, pug. I'm sorry."

His sigh expressed a weariness she could identify with. Her own nerves felt frayed and raw. She realized she was trembling. "I want to go to the hospital."

"I imagine the whole Dalton clan will be there. Let me report in to headquarters, then I'll drive you down."

In the city she and Adam waited with the rest of the family while Zack was in recovery. He'd already been through surgery and the damage repaired. Beau reported that all was well.

"Who were the men who shot him?" Roni asked, looking bewildered. "Hired guns? Hired to do what?"

"Find me," Honey told her, "and make me lead them to Adam."

"Did you know, when you came with Zack to the ranch, that they were after you?"

Honey nodded.

Roni's gaze grew indignant. "You were the cause of Zack getting shot," she accused.

"Hush, girl," Uncle Nick said quietly.

But Honey already knew she was to blame. Guilt

sat heavily on her shoulders as they waited, she and Adam seated on one sofa in the narrow room, the Dalton family aligned on the other side of the scarred coffee table. It was a gulf as wide as Hells Canyon.

"Honey?" Beau said, coming into the silent waiting room. "Zack is asking for you. I think he needs to see that you're okay."

Honey was aware of the eyes on her back as she left the room and followed Beau down the hall.

Chapter Fourteen

After seeing Zack and assuring him she was fine, then finding out his wound hadn't done major harm and he would be dismissed the next day if his vital signs were still strong, Honey felt her presence wasn't needed at the hospital. She asked Adam to drive her back to Lost Valley. They arrived shortly before sunrise.

She slept until noon, then went to the community center for the matinee performance at three. Everyone was full of questions about Zack and the shoot-out. Honey explained as briefly as she could.

"I just heard the news on the local radio station. The hit men were after you and your brother?" Danny questioned when he arrived, looking impressed and envious of her role in the arrests. "Way cool, man!"

Amelia rolled her eyes. "We have a show to put on. Let's get to it."

Later, dining with Adam at the lakeside restaurant, Honey learned that Zack had been safely transported to the ranch around noon. All the cousins were there, too, including Beau, who had assisted in the surgery.

"That's good," she said. "He's in good hands."

"I'll take you out there after the show this evening."

She shook her head. "It'll be late. Everyone will be asleep. I can see Zack another time."

But she had already thought this through during the long hours of the night. Zack was going to be okay, so there was no need for her to hover over him. It was time to leave this valley.

Roni had been right. She'd brought nothing but trouble with her. If Zack had been killed... She couldn't bear to think about it.

Adam gave her a pinch on the arm to bring her thoughts back to them. "Are you going to run away?"

"No, but I don't see any point in hanging around. I don't think the dance-studio idea will work."

"You haven't given it a try."

She gave him a troubled glance. "Do you think I should stay?"

"I think you should go for it." Adam grinned. "You were brave last night. Don't be a coward today. Zack is a cop. Getting shot goes with the territory. His cousin knows that. She was just upset last night."

''She had a right to be. I knew I wasn't the lost cousin, yet I came here, using them for my own purposes. All of them have been incredibly kind, actually.''

''You came at my insistence,'' he reminded her. ''You need to talk to Zack before making any drastic decisions. I think he wants you to stay close. Tell him that as your brother, I expect an offer of marriage to be forthcoming.''

The waitress, the same one they'd had last week, glanced from one to the other at the mention of marriage as she set their plates on the table.

''Not me,'' Adam told the girl with an amused glance. ''Marriage isn't part of my future.''

She gave him a flirtatious smile, one filled with challenge. ''It might not be so bad with the right person. Maybe you just haven't met her yet.''

''Maybe not,'' he agreed with a sardonic laugh.

Honey managed a smile at their joking. After the woman left them, she sighed. She had one more show to get through before she could think about personal affairs. ''I think I'll go to the B and B and rest for a while.''

''Good idea. I'll catch tonight's show, then tomorrow I'm out of here.''

Her heart dipped to a new low. ''Where are you going? Do you have another case already?''

''I have to return to L.A. The district attorney's office will need a full report. I'll have to testify in the case. You and Zack might be called when it goes to trial.''

''I hadn't thought about that.''

''It'll be months.'' Adam grimaced. ''You know how the wheels of justice grind.''

''Slowly,'' she said.

Adam rose. ''Go see Zack tomorrow. You need to take his car to him. One of the twins can drive you back to town. If you come back.''

The performance that night went off with only one hitch—Romeo fell off the ladder as he and Juliet sang a duet. The audience applauded loudly.

Honey still hadn't made up her mind on the wisest course of action when the musical was over. Adam told her and Amelia goodbye and got on the road.

''Does he always disappear into the night?'' Amelia asked, her gaze thoughtful as they watched him leave.

''Always,'' Honey said, pasting on a smile. She'd never told Adam how it wrenched her heart each time he'd had to leave after one of his quick visits. She was a big girl now. She'd learned long ago not to cry over what couldn't be changed. ''Let's join the party, shall we?''

She and Amelia went back into the community center, where the cast party, complete with champagne as promised by Danny, was under way. For two hours, she smiled amid the thanks and congratulations, then she and Amelia returned to the Victorian. In her room, she put aside pretense of a courage she didn't feel. The tears came.

On Sunday morning Honey had just finished breakfast when Amelia brought a portable phone to her. "Uncle Nick," she mouthed, handing it over.

"Hello," Honey said, making her tone cheerful.

"When are you going to get out here?" he asked without preamble. "Zack is threatening to walk to town since he can't get anyone to drive him."

"Uh-oh, shall I bring his car out?" Honey asked him.

"You'd better bring yourself," he said, "pronto."

"I'll get on the road right away," she promised, and hung up. "Zack needs his car," she said to Amelia, who was filling up the muffin platter. "I'll take it to him."

"Take him a dozen of these poppy-seed muffins, too. They're his favorites. I'll fix a box for him if you'll give me a couple of minutes."

So it was that Honey found herself on the road to the ranch in Zack's car, a big bakery box of goodies on the seat beside her. She tried to think what she would say to him, but her mind refused to cooperate. As she neared the house, her heart beat harder and harder.

"Hi, where's Adam?" Roni greeted her at the door, peering over Honey's shoulder.

"He left last night. He had to get back to L.A. That's where his office is."

The cousin frowned. "What a louse," she said, then, "Zack's in his bedroom. You'd better go see him."

Honey was relieved to find no one in the living room. She'd thought she would have to run the gauntlet of the Dalton cousins before seeing Zack. Uncle Nick was in the kitchen. She gave him the box of muffins and received a hearty hug.

"Go on," he said, giving her a gentle shove.

By now her heart had slowed to a desperate thud that nearly shook her whole body as she walked down the hall. Zack's room was the first on the left. She paused at the open door and took a deep breath.

"About damn time," he called out.

She stepped into the room, which was definitely masculine in its decor of blue and tan with wood paneling halfway up the wall. A television sat on top of an old-fashioned highboy, its picture on but the sound off.

"Hi," she said.

"Come'ere," he growled.

She went to the bed. With his left hand, he tugged her down beside him. "Where have you been?"

"In town. The musical went well yesterday—"

That was as far as she got before he hooked a hand behind her neck and kissed her with such searing passion her resolve melted into a puddle at her feet.

"I've missed you," he told her, nibbling at her ear and throat. "So all went well with the show?"

"Yes."

He invited her to tell him all about it. She was still chattering nervously when Uncle Nick came in with a plate of muffins, a huge glass of milk and two mugs of coffee. He set the treat down, gave them an approving glance and said, "We'll all be outside for a while."

Zack nodded and looked pleased. "Wonder how much time alone we'll have?" He reached for her.

She evaded his embrace by catching his hand in both hers. "We're not going to make love," she told him.

"Not yet," he agreed, his eyelashes drooping sexily over those blue eyes.

Honey forced herself to breathe deeply. "Adam had to go back to L.A."

"Yeah, he called me this morning."

Honey blinked in surprise. "He did?"

"He said I'd better get things straightened out between us before you left. Are you thinking of skipping out?"

It was time, she thought. She had to answer honestly. "I'm thinking of leaving, yes. The town isn't really big enough to support a dance studio all year."

The good-natured cheer left his face. "Have you thought about us?"

She clenched her hands, realized she still held his

hand between hers and let go. He lifted her chin so she had to meet his gaze.

"It wouldn't work," she said.

"Why not?"

Thinking was nearly impossible. "You shouldn't need someone. You shouldn't depend on them because…"

"Because it hurts when they have to leave?" he finished for her. "I'm never going to leave you. I don't want you to leave, either."

"You were nearly killed because of me."

He shrugged her fear aside. "That's my job."

The tension hummed like an electric current between them in the silence that ensued.

"That's it, isn't it?" he murmured. "You're afraid something will happen. The way it did to your parents. How old were you when Adam left your aunt's house?"

"It doesn't matter. All right, I was eight," she admitted when he frowned.

"Everyone you've ever loved has left you," he said slowly, as if thinking it out as he spoke. "Your parents. Your brother. Then you had to give up the one thing you loved, your dancing, and go into hiding. Life's been tough on you, little girl," he ended, his tone soft.

"I don't need your pity," she told him, furious and miserable and determined to put an end to this foolishness.

"How about my love?" he asked in a harder tone. "Will you take that? Otherwise I sure as hell don't know what to do with it."

"You've only known me a month. How can you be sure it's l-love?" She hated the little stutter over the word.

"How can you be sure it isn't?" he demanded with pure male logic.

"Danger can make things seem different, much more intense than they actually are."

"How many men have you trusted enough to go off with them to a place you'd never heard of?"

"You were a lawman. Adam said I needed a safe place."

"You found it. With me. In my arms." He ran a fingertip over her cheeks and lips, then smoothed a lock of hair back from her temple. "You intrigued me from that first meeting. The feeling has only grown stronger the past month. When I uncovered the mystery that surrounded you, I found a woman of unusual courage, willing to do whatever it took to protect those she loved. That's the woman I want for my wife, for the mother of my kids."

She shook her head.

He sighed and gave her an exasperated perusal. "You'll have to get over the stubbornness. We Daltons have cornered the market on that."

"That's true," Roni said, walking in on them.

Honey had been concentrating so hard on what was

happening between her and Zack, she hadn't heard the cousins return to the house. From the living room, she heard several males exclaiming over the muffins and obviously helping themselves.

"Amelia sent those to me," Zack yelled at them.

"Too late," Roni advised. "Well? Are you two getting married or what?"

"We're still at the 'or what' stage," Zack said.

"Uncle Nick is going to be mad. He likes things settled," she explained to Honey. "Are you upset because of what I said at the hospital? I'm truly sorry about that. I know none of this was your fault. It was your brother's. I'll tell him so next time I see him." She grinned, then fell serious. "You'd better agree and put Zack out of his misery. He's really in love this time."

"Thanks for your help," he said dryly. "If you'll kindly depart, maybe we can work this out."

"Huh, you don't seem to be doing all that great on your own. Okay, I'm leaving," she added when he grabbed a pillow with his good hand and heaved it across the room.

"Are you two engaged yet?" Trevor asked, appearing at the door, half-eaten muffin in hand.

Zack groaned. "Will you get out of here?"

Honey realized she needed to take things in her own hands. "Give us five minutes," she requested, then closed the door on the grinning cousins.

Returning to her seat on the bed, she touched the

face of her beloved. "I do love you," she told him. "It scares me, but I can't deny it. However, maybe we should wait on the marriage idea for a while. To give us more time to know each other," she added when he started shaking his head.

"There's this piece of property for sale on the lake. It won't stay on the market for long. We need to move on this. It has to be marriage, and the sooner the better."

Honey tried to digest these seemingly unrelated topics. "You have to be married to buy this property?" she asked wryly.

"Well, it is a family-type home." He smiled happily. "Say yes, then we can kiss for four minutes before the others burst in."

Honey tried to think. She'd learned long ago not to be impulsive or accept life at face value, but the look in Zack's eyes—those heavenly blue Dalton eyes— burned away her worries, leaving only joy arching over them like a golden rainbow. She could trust this man, she realized, with her heart and with her dreams.

"It's okay," he told her softly. "We'll be together through thick and thin, for better or for worse—"

"Well?" Uncle Nick said impatiently from the other side of the door.

Zack looked into her eyes. She took a deep breath and nodded, knowing she could never turn her back on this man.

"It's settled," Zack called out.

Uncle Nick entered the room. He came to the bed and took each of them by the hand. Tears glistened in his eyes as he smiled at them. ''All things happen for the best,'' he assured them. ''Didn't I tell you so last year?''

''Last year?'' Honey was confused.

''I was, uh, involved with someone, but it was nothing,'' Zack told her, ''just a dress rehearsal for the real thing.''

''I'll go tell the rest.'' Uncle Nick hurried out, his step as frisky as a newborn lamb.

From the living room, they heard laughter and shouts of congratulations. ''I told you it wouldn't be more than a month,'' Trevor declared in satisfaction. ''Let's see, Travis owes me five, Beau owes me one, the cheapskate, and Seth owes me five…''

''When you marry me,'' Zack warned, ''you get the whole Dalton gang.''

''It's going to be fun—another page from my Wild West adventure,'' she murmured. ''I'll have to write all this down for our children and *their* cousins.''

Zack pulled her close. ''We know how this story ends—'and they lived happily ever after.' Does that sound about right to you?''

''It sounds exactly right.''

He kissed her tenderly. ''Uncle Nick was right. Everything happens for the best. You're the best thing that's ever happened to me,'' he whispered huskily.

"My good-luck piece. Let's go to Vegas and get married."

"No, here," she requested, "where my heart found its home." She looked at him with all the love she felt inside.

"Here, then," he agreed.

She opened the door and the cousins poured in, bringing a wealth of happiness in their laughter and congratulations.

More than a haven, she thought. Here was heaven itself, maybe only a little piece, but it was hers and Zack's to share. Forever.

* * * * *

Which Dalton gets advice
from Uncle Nick next?
Well, let's just say this time
the doctor is following orders!

Look for Beau's story this June!

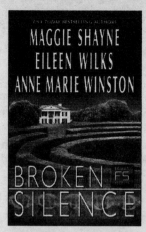

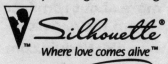

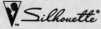

If you enjoyed what you just read,
then we've got an offer you can't resist!

Take 2 bestselling love stories FREE!

Plus get a FREE surprise gift!

Clip this page and mail it to Silhouette Reader Service™

IN U.S.A.	IN CANADA
3010 Walden Ave.	P.O. Box 609
P.O. Box 1867	Fort Erie, Ontario
Buffalo, N.Y. 14240-1867	L2A 5X3

YES! Please send me 2 free Silhouette Special Edition® novels and my free surprise gift. After receiving them, if I don't wish to receive anymore, I can return the shipping statement marked cancel. If I don't cancel, I will receive 6 brand-new novels every month, before they're available in stores! In the U.S.A., bill me at the bargain price of $3.99 plus 25¢ shipping and handling per book and applicable sales tax, if any*. In Canada, bill me at the bargain price of $4.74 plus 25¢ shipping and handling per book and applicable taxes**. That's the complete price and a savings of at least 10% off the cover prices—what a great deal! I understand that accepting the 2 free books and gift places me under no obligation ever to buy any books. I can always return a shipment and cancel at any time. Even if I never buy another book from Silhouette, the 2 free books and gift are mine to keep forever.

235 SDN DNUR
335 SDN DNUS

Name	(PLEASE PRINT)	
Address	Apt.#	
City	State/Prov.	Zip/Postal Code

* Terms and prices subject to change without notice. Sales tax applicable in N.Y.
** Canadian residents will be charged applicable provincial taxes and GST.
All orders subject to approval. Offer limited to one per household and not valid to current Silhouette Special Edition® subscribers.
® are registered trademarks of Harlequin Books S.A., used under license.

SPED02   ©1998 Harlequin Enterprises Limited

COMING NEXT MONTH